HOTTER THAN PUCK

MAINE MAULERS HOCKEY SERIES

ZOE BETH GELLER

KINKY INK PUBLISHING

Hotter Than Puck
Maine Maulers Hockey Romance Book 3

By Zoe Beth Geller

You can also follow me on Facebook and Amazon.

Please visit my website at zoegellerauthor.com

PLAY LIST OF HOTTER THAN PUCK

Playlist

Forever After All-Luke Combs
Shiver-Ed Sheeran
Kiss the Girl-Brent Morgan
Truth About You-Mitchell Tenpenny
At the End of the Bar- Chris Young,Mitchel Tenpenny
Drunk Me-Mitchell Tenpenny
Girl in It-Ray Fulcher

1

BLAKE

It's 67 degrees out when I stretch my tanned legs and head outside for my morning run. I can use the Maulers' training facility for this, but I'm digging my new neighborhood in Camden Hills, to be honest. So, why not?

I inhale the smell of the first fallen autumn leaves from the maple and oak trees as they flutter behind me on the sidewalk as I jog. Maine is still warm in August, and Lobsterfest, as is training camp, is just around the corner. I believe I can train in the outside environment, and it can be as good as, if not better, than pushing equipment. Everyone can attest to Rocky Balboa doing it in the movies, plus it's a productive way to learn about my surroundings.

I passed my neighbor's house, where I had not noticed any signs of life. No car in the driveway, no curtains drawn, and no lights on at night. It's even more bizarre that I notice coming from LA, a bustling place. But Maine has an entirely different feel to it. I don't notice it in a creepy neighbor—serial killer kind of way. I find it unusual for my suburban, upscale neighborhood, where I wave to cars coming and going with each run no matter what time it is. However, most people aren't up and out this early.

I make my way around another cul de sac and head to the clubhouse, where they have a restaurant, gym, and golf course. The golf course reminds me of the charity event on St. Bart's. I'm attending next week, and I still don't have a word about my new assistant from the agency. I need one to keep my life in order, and not having someone on board causes me anxiety.

Plus, it would be nice to get a round of golf or some bonding experience with the team before the season starts, but I need the assistant to set everything up. Not to mention, I don't want to worry about all the things I'm not great at keeping track of, like expenses, contacts, and especially my hotel room number.

I want this new person to be able to travel with me, but most of their job will be local. Part of my distraction from being unable to do simple tasks is that I'm always rehashing games in my head. That doesn't leave much room for details that are painfully memorable to others but totally foreign to me.

I run for an hour and make up some suicide drills in an empty parking lot. I lift some weights in the empty clubhouse gym. It's well after nine when I head back home. The neighborhood seems so normal and yet, not as friendly as I imagined it would be. After a week, I figured I'd meet with more than just a few teammates.

I come upon the Applewood Lane street sign, and as I get closer to my house, I notice a taxi in the mysterious neighbor's, usually vacant, driveway. A cab driver gets out and pulls two huge suitcases from the trunk. A woman hands him a tip before she lugs her bags behind her and struggles to get to the front door. That's a lot of stuff, considering the airlines charge extra for two bags, and I would love to know where she's been.

It's hard to see her figure hidden by the fake Louis Vuitton luggage, but curiosity gets the best of me when her honey-blonde hair falls over her shoulder. I figure, I can be a good neighbor and help her. I pick up my pace. She uses a hand and flips her long hair back, as it's impeding her vision, and I observe her tapping on the keyless entry.

I run to close the distance between us so I can say hello, but she slips through the door before I reach her.

Damn.

For all I know, she's married. And just because I'm on a break from relationships doesn't mean I can't look or dip my toe in the dating pond. One date doesn't mean I'm getting serious, but it might be a good idea to steer clear of dating the neighbor in any event. That's kind of like dating a co-worker. Everyone knows not to do it, but does that stand in their way once hormones take over?

Nope.

I want to say I'm not likely to make a mistake, but every athlete has a bad day. I think I left my last "mistake" in California and the idea that my mother left me as a young teen with my best interest at heart. Yeah, okay.

I slow my pace and walk past my house to cool down before doubling back to let myself in my house. These electronic front door locks are the latest technology, simplifying life with one less thing to keep track of.

Curiosity gets the best of me as I want to meet this mysterious neighbor. Like, who is that babe next door? Better yet, maybe I can make an accidental meeting look casual. I can't pretend to bleed out. That's overly dramatic. Maybe scope out her place and catch her the next time she comes out?

I'm thinking I sound like a stalker, but maybe she'll be out later. She lives next door. How hard can that be?

I'm sure I'm just horny, and my need to meet her will be gone by morning.

I peel off my running shirt and use it to wipe the sweat off my back and chest as I make my way to the state-of-the-art kitchen. It's decked out in whites, grays, and wood flooring throughout, giving it warmth.

I chug down a blue Gatorade as I was raised on it, and it's my favorite flavor. It doesn't hurt they sponsor tons of teams across the country, making sure all team benches are loaded with towels plastered with their logo, but they also hand them out at fundraisers.

I've been too alone this past week, but pre-season is just around the corner, and it's a terrible time to meet a girl. I'm not about to commit my life to anyone or anything other than hockey. Eventually, I will meet the guys on the team, and we'll bond after numerous practices and alcohol. I want to fit in with my new team. This is a fresh start for me as I won't have to worry about running into my ex-girlfriend.

I'm not relationship material. That was the one takeaway from the breakup with Ashley. I can act the part, sure. But I can't see myself falling in love. I have yet to feel real heartache from a love lost, and I doubt I'm even capable of it, given my childhood filled with anger issues towards my mother. I have difficulty trusting anyone other than my agent, Dan, and my brother, Sam. Sam is in college and playing football.

Ashley didn't seem to care that I was emotionally unavailable in the beginning. She seemed wrapped up in her career and loved me on her arm. Rumor had it she was ready to shop for a wedding dress. In my mind, we're too young and haven't screwed up or made enough mistakes to know who our mate for life should be. Maybe I'm not cut out for married life.

Dating used to be fun way back when hookups were more acceptable because we were immature and boisterous. It seems the more successful we become as athletes, the easier it is for girls to find us, and then the harsh reality hits—jocks don't have to look for hot women. Women find us like heat-seeking missiles.

2

RACHEL

"Charlotte, you really shouldn't. . ." She interrupts me as she slides money into my hand.

"Stop, what are best friends for? If things work out for you in Maine, I can sublet your half of the apartment. That way, you won't have to continue paying rent."

"You make it sound like we're breaking up," I tease to cover my sadness. She knows I hate to ask for favors, but rent is a huge expense. "It's nice my brother offered to help."

"Yes, it is. I like him much more since he's been with Callie. And don't worry, the shitstorm here will blow over. Promise." Charlotte helps me get my luggage out of the trunk of her car, and we pass it to the airport skycap.

If anyone can survive this fiasco, I can. I went last year eating mostly ramen noodles. I was so broke I only eat meat once a week, so yeah, I can do this. When things were great and my career flourished, I could afford to live a comfortable life. Then, shit happened, and I ended up jobless. It wasn't my fault this time. But failure still stings. I'm the loser in the family. My endless list of jobs is peppered with one disappointment after another.

Fuck Joel.

Only he fucked me over first. Just when I could finally afford to splurge on an espresso and a slice of decadent tiramisu from the Michelin-star restaurant the parental units took me to for my birthday in January, he fucked me. God, I love Italian food and would love to eat there again.

I hug Charlotte. "I don't know when I'll see you."

"It won't be long. It's roughly a four-hour drive and only one border. Besides, you'll get to know all your brother's hockey buddies, and who knows what will happen? Remember, you need to get under a hot, sweaty hunk to gather those steamy love scenes for that breakout novel. I can't wait for you to finish it so I can edit it." She hugs me, and we both realize I'm starting a new chapter. I choke back sobs at the thought of leaving my country, best friend, and mentor.

Most of the time, men make us change our living arrangements. Understandably, if one of us were to get serious with a guy, the next logical step would be living together or getting engaged. Until then, our independent lives revolved around our family or best friends.

"Thanks for the lift. Thanks for everything." My voice cracks, and I wipe a tear off my cheek before I pull away from her.

"I'll see you soon." She blows me a kiss, then hops in her car. I watch her pull away as if she is my only lifeline. She would have been if my brother didn't make some calls for me. He found me a job and is letting me crash at his place.

I'm thankful the Skycap is here to help because I don't have the patience to use a kiosk. Every time I fly, it's something different. One time, it's a credit card. The next time? It will be a barcode. What's next, a retina scan? A brain biopsy? Whatever. I tip the man for saving me the aggravation, and he lets me know what gate to go to after the security checkpoint.

Once inside the terminal, I remember I've been prescreened, so I advance to the front of the line. After the security checkpoint, I wait at the gate for my short flight from Quebec to Maine. I'm relieved my brother was traded. He's closer to home, having moved from Phoenix, where he played for the Diamondbacks. Now he's with the Maulers. I'm thrilled I'll see more of him.

I kill time watching the news on the overhead monitor and zone out until I see my brother's wedding picture come on the screen with the caption *Honeymoon in Hawaii*. Yes, Quebec loves its newest golden boy. The red carpet is rolled out for him when he comes home. He was touched by the gods regarding his looks and skills. I hope his kids inherit that, too.

I'll be on my own at his place for a week while they finish their honeymoon, and my brother said he left me money for food and the keys to Callie's car if I need it. I'm not sure if I need a special license to drive in Maine. I know Canadians travel to the States all the time, and many have second houses there, mostly in warm weather locations like Florida. But Maine, sheesh, I wish I was somewhere warmer.

If my wishes were to come true, my brother would play for a team with warmer weather than Maine. Quebec is still on the East Coast, so at least it's a direct flight.

How nice for Alexandre that he is in Hawaii. He cashed in on the vacation time while he could because he and Callie are going to be tied down with their newborn after the New Year. Alexandre got a last-minute deal, too, and they left immediately after a small wedding. He'll barely make it home in time for training camp.

I hear an announcement calling for my row to board and join the line. Once I'm on the plane, I check my seat number for the tenth time. Funny, I have no problem navigating the internet, but don't expect me to remember my seat number. Forget it. My short-term memory sucks.

I find my row and sit at the window with my backpack in my lap. I always travel with a change of underwear, phone, computer charger, allergy pills, and silver laptop—I call her Belle.

Is it weird to name a device? People name their cars. I don't own a car, so I think it's fair. But as for the underwear, it's insurance that my luggage won't be lost. Who wants to be stuck wearing the same underwear for two days?

Ew.

I should be working on my novel, the novel that's taking forever to finish. I'm upset and still reeling from being dropped from the lucrative makeup sponsorships. It was a great gig, and it paid my bills so I could finish my novel without working a nine-to-five job and commuting. The only problem is that the job was still a time suck, and the novel is unfinished.

People stow their carry-ons and take their seats around me. I tune out the distractions. It's easy to do; I have the window, and that's all I care about. The pilot announces we have clearance for take-off. We taxi off the runway, and I take one last look at Quebec as we fly out.

Once airborne, I sit back and put in my earbuds. I experience a twinge of anxiety that my brother thinks I'm qualified to be an assistant for someone. I don't know what kind of cornflakes he's eating. I don't know what I'll be doing, and I doubt I'll like taking orders from someone. I'm used to working on my own.

Besides, I have no idea what the players' schedules are like. I'm sure they all have contractual things to follow. Beyond that, I'm clueless about the rest of the rules. From being around Alexandre, I saw first-hand how they like to party and throw drinks back like they are vitamins.

They prank each other all the time with drink concoctions they call "Icing" and different disgusting mixtures like buzz balls. No clue, but it sounds disgusting. However, the guys are a family at the end of the day. Alexandre says the Maulers remind him of what he had with his travel teams before graduating high school. This means his team is very close because he's still in touch with most of the guys he played with years ago.

Callie warned me that some of the girlfriends and wives could be "a handful," as she put it. Not to worry, you won't see me dating a professional athlete. They are all players, on and off the ice.

Alexandre said he and his friends hooked up with all my girlfriends over the years. Much to my dismay, I realize now that most of those girls might have been my friends so they could get an easy access pass to the handsome players.

Nothing like women throwing panties at guys. It sends them a message they can't refuse. Ironically, I also discovered my brother shut down any dating of his sister. I wondered why I never had a date in high school. It's such a double standard.

I wonder if my life would have been different if I had a serious relationship with a classmate. I never felt attractive my entire high school career. I'm nothing special as far as looks. I have boobs and a curvy ass. I can apply makeup like a professional.

My social media following is a testament to my ability to commercialize my talents with makeup skills and tips. But I am always Alexandre's little sister. Even my parents idolize him and worry about me. I'm still trying to find myself and prove I can be successful, too.

No matter what happens next, I'm confident Callie will have my back now that we're officially family.

She told me all the hockey girlfriends vie for an engagement ring. I don't know why women put so much emphasis on being engaged. Supposedly engagement rings mean everything to the women who date pro athletes. No matter the sport, it carries weight.

Pfft.

I'm not impressed by status symbols. If I were, I would still be with Joel. He would have given me anything I wanted, but he wasn't the one. I don't have much, but I refuse to settle for someone just to be financially supported.

I still can't get over how Joel played me. I didn't see that coming. It just goes to show you never really know someone. How could I have been so stupid as to let him see my passwords when I logged into my social media accounts? I trusted him. I had no reason not to trash me the way he did. He was vindictive when I broke up with him.

When I failed to remember the date of our four-month anniversary, he must've figured out that I wasn't that into him.

I'm beginning to think Joel may have planned to destroy me if I ever left him. But to record us eating steaks the size of Montana and post it to my business account? That vindictive stuff right there.

He knows I am an influencer for pro-PETA makeup lines and against animal testing. On top of that, I have many followers who live a vegan lifestyle. Well, if that's not sheer betrayal, I don't know what is.

In one heartbeat, he effectively crashed my side hustle — which was my primary source of income. Literally, one heartbeat is all it took. Social media is immediate and unforgiving. The backlash can last forever. Just ask the beer company that tanked this year.

Not only was I canceled by my sponsors, but I've been vilified by others in the industry. I lost my business. Now, I have to find a way to survive and finish my novel. It's a new beginning for me, being an author. I imagined doing this since I was a child. I decided the events that transpired this past week might have a silver lining. I dusted off my manuscript and figured I might be on the path I'm supposed to take in life. Writing and reading are my passions.

My biggest roadblock to finishing this novel is writing the sex scenes because I've never had an all-consuming love. You know, the love that makes your knees weak. The love of a guy you can't wait to hear from and can't wait to be fucked by. Charlotte knows I've never had that kind of love or mind-blowing sex, and she said it shows in my writing. How can I write a romance novel when I'm lacking romance? I've never had a satisfying sex life.

Writers are supposed to write what they know best. I can't write what I have never experienced. The way my life has been of late, the only thing I'm qualified to write are horror stories.

Maybe Charlotte is on to something. Maybe a hockey hottie is what I need.

Just a fling, a one-night stand for research purposes. I don't want to be in a committed relationship. Joel had my future mapped out—from our joint incomes to what I would be doing for a work and he even planned out how many kids we'd have. Suffocating doesn't even begin to paint the picture I saw with him. How could I have been so naïve?

It's taken me years to get a college degree and realize that my gift is creative writing. It's hard to explain what it's like being a struggling author. It's almost impossible to explain to my parents what an influencer is and how I make money off people following me on social media. You'd think the word influencer was a dirty word from the looks on their faces.

Speaking of dirty, I wonder what the Maine Maulers will look like this year after the incredible and public defeat a few months ago. The team was booed exiting the ice. Their confidence must have been smashed to smithereens. I've been there myself; ironically, I don't play hockey.

I did figure skating only because my parents put me in classes to keep me busy while they watched Alexandre practice with his team. I had no interest in competing on the ice, even to garner my parents' attention. It wasn't all bad. During his games, I ate hotdogs, fries, and sodas.

I know my brother always focused on the prize and worked hard. I'm happy he made it all the way. The fact that he got more attention at home doesn't mean I love him any less. It's not his fault he got great genetics and that Mom and Dad love hockey. Growing up in that environment may explain why I tend to date anyone who shows me a hint of attention.

After I land in Maine, I take an Uber to my brother's house. I can't believe technology and that I must remember the code to open these new-fangled doors by punching buttons. I push the door in, and it works the first time—a small feat but a miracle all the same. I turn to grab my luggage and get a glimpse of a jogger who takes my breath away. I see him looking at me and quickly look away.

But not before taking a mental snapshot. He's wearing running shorts that show off his muscular thighs. His sleeveless shirt is wet and clings to him, showing his muscular torso and biceps. I want to stare; he's gorgeous. Instead, I close the door. I need to make sure he's in view when I sip my coffee tomorrow, preferably without his running shirt.

3
____

BLAKE

It's dark outside when I walk past the picture window and notice everyone on the street has garbage bins lined up like tin soldiers. That's my life, learning as I go. I hate to read a menu, let alone the fine print in my lease agreement.

I exit through the garage and make my way to the side of the house, grab my rolling garbage and recycle containers, one in each hand, and roll them at the same time. I don't create much trash, but plenty of wildlife would love to get into it. If I don't keep up with this, the raccoons will have it strewn all over the street. So here I am, in the middle of the night, keeping my neighbors happy like a model citizen.

Halfway to the curb, I hear the neighbor's front door open, and the screen door slam shut.

I drop my bins at the curb, turn, and wait. She's wearing a white bathrobe so long she's holding it up to avoid tripping. She's amusing, so I watch, waiting to see how this will play out. How long will the oversized robe stay on her shoulders with the way it's slipping off?

She grabs one bin, turns to roll it down the inclined driveway, and after she notices me, she gives me a quick smile.

I call out, "Forget it was trash night?"

"Almost! My brother asks very little of me. The least I can do is take out his trash."

"Your brother lives here?"

"Oh, yeah, he and his new wife. They're still trying to figure out which house to live in, out in the country just outside of town or this swanky mini-mansion. Seriously, does every house have three master bedrooms?"

"I imagine they do. So, you're just visiting?"

This is getting better and better. In a perfect world, she tells me she'll be leaving, so I don't have to worry about her expecting wedding bells and a white picket fence.

"Sort of, maybe. You?"

She drops her bin on the curb.

I never know what women want. But the ones that hang on like I'm the last lifeboat at the sinking of the Titanic tend to find me. What can I say? I'm a magnet for the desperate and delirious women that the guys refer to as "cling-on" or hitchhiker plant. They are named after those little green suckers that cling to your jeans before you realize you walked through a patch of them.

"Just moved in recently, a job thing," I answer. I've learned that less is more on a first meeting.

"Oh. Guess we'll be neighbors for a while." Her cheerful voice is as refreshing as cold lemonade on a summer day.

She turns to retrieve the second bin, so I walk with her. She's petite, and at 6'1", I tower over her. Instinctively, I have a need to help. So, when we get to her trash can, I grab it first. My chivalrous side comes from my country's upbringing— respect your elders and women. The creed is to treat them right and be always polite.

One-night stands are not my thing, and it's probably why I get stuck in relationships that go nowhere. But, if this is just a temporary residence for her, this might work out perfectly for me. No permanency is implied.

"You don't have to do that," she tries to brush me off.

"It's fine. What are neighbors for?" I insist.

We walk to the curb together, and we chat when a gust of wind blows the top of the recycling bin up. She lets go of her robe to catch the lid, and her robe slips open, revealing a beautiful breast lit by the full moon just begging to be touched.

"Oops, it's my brother's robe, and he's much bigger than me. I wasn't expecting to meet anyone at this hour, y'know?" Her cheeks turn red.

She pulls her robe closed and folds her arms across her chest as if it's normal, but it's not. It's so awkward the only sound I hear is crickets.

I break the silence. "Don't worry. I didn't see a thing. I'm Blake, by the way," I say, extending my hand.

"Rachel." The touch of her dainty hand in mine fires all the synapses in my body. IT hits me like a hockey puck to the chest—hard. *Damn*, this chick has my attention, but something tells me she doesn't want it.

Baffled, I give her hand a gentle squeeze and let go.

Her long hair is blowing in the wind, and I detect the scent of wildflowers and honey. She pushes the hair away from her face and tucks it behind her ear.

"So, have you been to bars or nightclubs yet?" I ask.

"Not really. You?"

Her Nordic blue eyes are inquisitive. However, I'm not prepared for questions. I'm living life here as low-key as possible. She's on a need-to-know basis, and right now, I'm enjoying that she doesn't recognize me—nor does she need to know who I am.

"Nope. I haven't gotten very far into the social scene yet. How about we grab a beer? I mean, if you're free. I know it's last minute, and we just met."

"Umm, I don't know. I haven't been in the mood to go out," she says.

I chuckle. "That's when you need to go out. Do you know of a place?"

"I do. I don't know if you'll like it. We might run into some hockey players or Mauler fans, eh?" she had to mention the hockey guys.

"Really? Hockey players, you say." Crap, I don't want to run into players who will recognize me. I want to maintain my cover of obscurity for one night. Anonymous dating, if there is such a thing.

"I thought about going out, but it feels weird without my roommate who stayed in Quebec. . .."

"I hear there's a country bar in town. Are you into that?" I ask, taking over the arrangements.

I already know her distinct accent is from Quebec. I hang out with lots of French-speaking Canadians, and they have their particular dialect. If they haven't been taught English in school, they quickly pick it up on the road, just like the players from Russia.

"Country music is nice," she replies, her voice floating over me like feathers, soft and gentle like a summer breeze.

"I was going to check the Barrel Room tonight. If you're interested, you can join me. Then, neither of us has to go alone."

"Um." She pauses, clearly running through her options and worst-case scenarios.

I know the drill. Usually, there is a girlfriend to bring along for safety. Girls are like Noah's Ark. They travel in twos. It's wise to be safe and works well until one gets a boyfriend.

It's the same with the players when we collectively blow the girlfriend or wife off for a night out or an early tee time on the golf course with the guys.

"I don't know. You go, maybe I'll see you there."

I'm disappointed, sure. But I have hope. There's a possibility she'll come. My guess, she needs to talk to her girlfriend and weigh her options.

"Alright," I reply respectfully. "Nice meeting you..." and it's now that I realize I don't know her name.

"Rachel," she says.

"Blake," I reply, and I flash her the smile that usually wins a girl over.

"Well, nice meeting you," I reiterate and pause, hoping she'll change her mind.

"You too, Blake."

Hmm. She may not be a puck bunny, but she is familiar with the Maulers' hangout, which was more than I knew on my first day here.

"Night." She turns to go.

"Hey, if you come, beers are on me." I kick myself for nudging her with the invite again. I don't want to miss this opportunity because our chemistry is off the charts. I can't take my eyes off her. Is she experiencing the same connection? To me, it seems obvious.

"Okay." Her shy smile makes me melt like a popsicle on the Fourth of July.

I watch her walk away, finding the robe is a sexy look on her even though it doesn't show off her figure. The fact of her being naked underneath it makes me so hard that I could put a dent in my garage door.

I have no problem imagining what's under her robe, especially after seeing her white, firm, perky breasts. It's like the excitement of scoring a game-winning goal, only I'm horizontal and sporting wood. It's funny how the highs of both are incredible.

She disappears inside, and I fear she won't meet me. Especially after the noise of the front door lock clicking, and my heart sinks with it. Usually, I need to warm up to a woman before inviting her out, but Rachel is different. I'm at ease with her when she opens her succulent lips to speak.

I didn't plan on going out tonight. I just wanted a chance to get to know her. Now I'm stuck going out because I can't miss the possibility she might show up. It would be awkward for me to be caught in a lie.

No, it would suck. Besides, I do what I say. I'm reliable like that. It's probably from my dad bopping me upside the head if I fell behind in my schoolwork because I was online all night playing video games. "Consequences," he used to say. I knew he had my best interest at heart. All I wanted was to play video games and hockey.

I return inside my home and find myself going over what to wear like it's prom night. It would be comical if I weren't too old for first-date jitters. I'm older and have been to spiffy public engagements where everything is perfect, and the press takes pictures.

Tonight, I second guess my staple, dark blue dress shirt, but it accentuates the blue hues in my light eyes, gifts from my Norwegian and Irish ancestors. I have to go with it, and I know my buddies in California would agree. Damn, I'm twenty-three now. I need to dress myself.

My brown leather Lucchese boots fit like a glove, and girls love pulling them off me. What else does a dude wear to a country bar, anyway? It's a no-brainer.

Maine is farm country, and there are plenty of pickups. Old Red arrived yesterday by transport. The neighbors will love that in my driveway because the truck won't fit in the garage. They don't think of these things today, but this is just my temporary living situation until I see how things pan out with the team.

I want to drive my old truck to the country bar tonight and hope Rachel shows up. On the other hand, a sports car speaks volumes. The orange Charger impresses women, and I hit the garage door button with optimism in my chest. I'll warm her up in the driveway, and Rachel will hear it as it's a high-performance vehicle. Everyone on the street will hear the muffler when I drive down the road.

4

———

RACHEL

He said he'd be at the Bourbon Barrel Saloon. All I planned to do was watch an old Nicholas Sparks movie, watch Zac Efron walking around for two hours, and then get off on my vibrator as I fantasize about him. What self-respecting single woman doesn't have an electric vibrator and a hot stud to consider to get the deed done?

I'm such a loser. I should be living it up instead of spending my young adult life hiding in my brother's house. I do have work tomorrow, so I won't drink too much. I don't even like beer, but the reality is most guys do.

Charlotte told me to go live it up, and I can't finish my book without some hot, sweaty sex scenes. Blake is. . . well, he's more than capable of showing a gal a good time judging from the way his t-shirt stretched to show off how ripped he is. And his smile turned me inside out. I wanted to ask what he does for a living but shrugged it off. It doesn't matter. All that matters is that I accomplish my mission.

I would love it if he could bend me like he does that workout shirt's cotton and elastane fibers. I am sure I'd be a satisfied woman. What better way to write a scorching love scene than to hit the keys after a hot hookup? Maybe I can channel real-life events into my story. It's research, I tell myself.

Charlotte's right. I can't write what I don't know. I need to kick myself into gear if I'm to write anything worth reading. I turn the knob to my walk-in closet, and the recessed lights flicker on automatically. How cool is that?

I stare at my scantily clad rod that's holding twelve hangers in the most beautiful built-out closet. It's a shame I don't have pretty things to put in it. I didn't bring much. I don't have but one pair of boots. It will fall soon, and these boots screamed 'take me.'

I am a sucker for footwear. I like designer stuff like any woman but can't afford to buy it. Hence, the knockoffs. If I'm lucky, I find expensive items after they've run their course and go on clearance sections in expensive stores or peruse discount stores, hoping I'll find something in decent.

If the new job works out, I can have Charlotte ship me more of my clothes. I can also buy items locally once I get on my feet financially. This makes me chuckle. I have no clue where to shop in Maine. I'm doubtful it will have shopping like Quebec. But who knows? The city is growing, and the east coast usually means fashion if New York City is any indication. I know there are expensive homes on the coast of Maine, there must be shops worthy of my brother's income.

Pfft, I make the noise to soothe myself. I wish Charlotte were here to help. I'll figure something out as I look at the dreadful state of my practical clothing in front of me. Nothing says come fuck me better than heels, but I don't have any of those here. I packed sensible work shoes.

I hate that my brother put his name out to help me find a job so quickly. I need to make a good impression on my first birthday because he set a job up for me. I don't want to jeopardize his sterling reputation.

I click Charlotte's face on my phone to call her over video for free. Her phone rings a few times. Oh, God, I hope she's not doing it right now.

"What's up?" She answers on the fourth ring.

"You're home?"

"Yes, unfortunately. I'm drinking some wine and dancing to some tunes from the 90s. It's too quiet around this flat without you. How's it going?"

"Um. Good. Maybe?"

"Who'd you meet?"

Damn. I can never surprise her. She's more of a fucking crystal ball guru than she is human. I need to ask her about that one day. Her sixth sense has been on fire lately. She never liked Joel, as it turns out. It would have saved me the most embarrassing event of my entire life if she had clued me in. Social media is fun until shit happens, then your name is dirty like mine.

Charlotte said if I disappear until the trending story dies down, I could eventually start over. It was a lucrative job. However, now I think that job made me procrastinate on my love of writing. Living in Maine with my brother is a lateral move to buy me time to work out my myself. It also keeps me from having to move home a failure.

"A hot as fuck guy next door. Quite the looker."

"Oh, well, have you met?"

"Yes, and I was wearing Alexandre's robe and had a boob slip out—right in front of him at the curb. How embarrassing." My fast-talking explanation is delivered in one breath.

Her familiar laugh wanes in and out over the Wi-Fi for a second.

"Are you done laughing?" My stern tone should convey

the fact that I'm under pressure and in need of help. I'm in a tizzy over this dude who was sporting wood when he got close to me, and I'm more determined than ever to see if he's all he appears to be.

"This is my career on the line. I need to get laid if I'm to write worthy sex scenes." My reply reflects my desperate plea to be successful tonight. It's just a one-night stand. One and done, where's the harm in that?

Joel didn't have much of an imagination. Sex was boring to the point of me staring at the ceiling, wishing he didn't have that shot of tequila before leaving the restaurant as it makes him last forever. I wouldn't have minded if he had set my body on fire.

However, the chemistry never developed for me, so there is absolutely nothing to write about there. Now, I want to crucify him for his asshole behavior. Sex with anyone else has to be better than it was with him.

"Okay, relax, I'm good, really. That's priceless. Okay, so do you have a date? Or don't you?

Why does she ask so many questions? Ugh. This is why she's so good at writing copy and editing. Tonight, it's annoying. I wish she would wear her best friend's hat, not the 'I'm still working' one.

I've never had my world rocked by a man. I have an inkling Blake might change my pathetic love life. The fact that Blake made my body tremble when he moved closer to me is already giving me great research material.

Truthfully, I'm dying for some wicked, hot sex. I have a high sex drive but want to test my theory.

I doubt I was ever to Joel. Sex was the last thing on my mind with him. I just wanted to roll over and get some sleep since I had long days taping and editing videos. What I want and need is earth-shattering sex, sex that will have me drooling and pass the final cut for the novel that would make an R-rated movie if it ever made it to the box office.

"He invited me out for beers at a country bar, and I told him maybe I'd meet him there."

"Did you have chemistry with him? That is always a must for the hottest sex. But you know what? It doesn't matter. You need your research, and you need to get laid. You're gorgeous, he's hot. Go for it!"

"You mean like I'm wet as a road with melted ice, and instead of a pothole in front of me, it's his light blue eyes that draw me in like I'm never going to return to earth?"

"Wow." She's silent for a moment. I can tell by her face I'm on to something. She's in shock. Her jaw drops.

What does this mean? Is it bad?

"That's it," her tone is soft but definitive. "Okay," she shifts gears and her attitude. "Good job. You totally lucked into it. Go out with him. Don't wait for him to question if you're interested. Men like that have women lined up. Just remember, it's research. No commitment, no attachments, just a fling. Go for it and ride him for all it's worth. Don't hate yourself in the morning unless the sex sucks. He's definitely into you to ask you out so quickly."

"Fine. Samantha. . ." I agree with what she's saying. I know she's a pushover for a man with a good set of balls, I mean eyes, and a big dick. She's got every man she's gone after. The reference to *Sex and the City's* Samantha nails her perfectly.

"Just remember, if the guy is popular, there's a reason. Especially if a man isn't the best in the looks department, it means he's either loaded or has an exceptional dick."

"Ugh. No, he's not lacking in the looks department." I sigh. "Now, focus. What do I wear?"

"Not the robe." She snickers.

"This is serious. It's my future career as a writer is on the line. I need to know what will turn him on."

"Wear skinny jeans, heels or boots, and a shirt that has one too many buttons undone. Show some cleavage, and just be yourself. I'm sure he'll be all in."

"Really?"

"You have him on the hook. Besides, you called me, didn't you?"

"Point taken. All right. I'm going."

"And don't spend an hour doing your makeup like a professional. Just put on bronzer and lipstick and waltz out. Men hate to be kept waiting."

"You're kidding, right?" Me, without makeup? How did I fall so far so quickly?

"No. He liked you with nothing on, and if the night goes well, you'll be out of those clothes in no time. Call me tomorrow. But run, don't give another woman time to pick up your man!"

"Fine." I take it as a personal challenge to resist my temptation with the eyelash curler and the pore minimizer. "I'm on it. Call you later?"

"Good luck, eh?"

"Yep." I click the phone off.

Shit. What do I wear?

I pull a random button-down shirt off the hanger with such force the hanger rocks before flipping off the wooden bar. I remove my jeans from the pant hanger. I'm a girl. How did my brother end up with the designer closet? He has the best of everyting. I'm fucking Cinderella without the clothes or the carriage. However, I have a hot fucking man who wants to see me tonight.

The shoe rack is pathetic. I have low heels for work, a

pair of sneakers (because that just seemed logical for Maine), and one pair of black fashion boots.

Country bar—boots it is. I'm into it as I grab them from my near-empty closet. I tug them on before I enter my bathroom because all the rooms here are master bedrooms. I've never seen anything like it.

These hockey players sure know how to live.

I apply a few strokes of bronzer to my fair complexion, outline my lips, and apply Forever Love red lipstick. I step back from the huge mirror and fluff out my hair. It's become curly with the humidity in the air, but straightening it would take too much time.

I look in the mirror and decide this is as good as it gets for the short notice. I undo one button on my blouse and more and feel like a slut, so I re-button it. He knows what they look like. I doubt I have to remind him as I cringe at the replay.

I grab my tiny purse loaded with only the necessities and snag Callie's car keys off the hook as I make my way out the door to the garage. Here goes nothing that I hope will be something.

The bar is dark as I enter, and the heavy wooden door creaks as it closes behind me. My eyes adjust to the dim atmosphere. The speakers reflect the voice of the band's lead singer on the stage with a microphone in his hand.

He's country all right, with the western hat, dark blue denim jeans, and brown cowboy boots. I can tell by the way he moves that he must work in his worn jeans. Shiny boots are expensive and dressy, his are not. He's got a great voice, and it seems like everyone here knows him as they walk to the small stage and put money in his tip jar.

Heads turn when I walk in. I push my shoulders back to give the air of confidence, but when so many men look my way, I worry I popped a button on my blouse. I slide my lithe fingers down over my buttons and boobs to make sure I'm not flashing again.

My nose is confronted with the pungent smell of soured beer as I linger around the long and narrow bar. The wooden chairs are filled with men who are much too old to date. They look like they are at home on the barstools. I can't erase the sight of their wide butts as they spill over the small circular wood stool they are sitting on, and I am privy to seeing more butt cracks than if I were standing at a construction site.

This is clearly not my scene, but then I remind myself everyone makes sacrifices for the love of their creative careers, and I'm not bailing now. The book is my only redeeming event in my control, and I will make it happen come hell or high water.

This bar appears to be the watering hole for the locals, all right. I'm underwhelmed, to say the least. I'm in a quandary when I don't see Blake. I question turning around to leave because I don't fit in. I'm about to panic when my name rises over the noise, greeting my ears like a warm cup of tea on the coldest day of the year.

Blake. He's here. I breathe a sigh of relief.

Blake inches closer to me without turning as the fresh evergreen and woodsy scents float with his movement. He sucks me in like a smoking rotisserie hot dog at a picnic.

I blink to recover from my swoon fest and notice the beer mug in his hand. I'm dizzy, which is impossible. I've not even had a drink. I'm about to stumble on the concrete floor that must be uneven because I've never tripped in these boots. I'm not clumsy. I'm convinced it's the floor.

"Hi." I can't help but smile as I glance up at him as he towers over me. He's a sight to behold with his light blond hair that's slicked back. I pick up the musky bergamot in his cologne. His essence is so delightful my pussy quivers and yearns to be touched.

"Glad you made it. I have a table closer to the dance floor," his enthusiasm is contagious, especially when he flashes me his smile, and I'm willing to follow him anywhere, even if my knees are weak.

"Great." I can't contain the excitement in my voice or my lacy undies as he slips his hand up my back, and it rests between my shoulder blades as if to say it's 'hands off' as he gently guides me through the growing crowd.

All eyes in the room are glued on us, and it's strange. Why would anyone be looking at me? He's the gorgeous one, and I'm nobody. So, it has to be him. I'm happy to be here and not at home sulking over my washed-up bank account that's currently negative.

"You look great," he whispers in my ear as the band hits a few instruments to warm up for another set. Currently, the male singer is talking to the crowd. Apparently, it's not a break time, and the evening is just starting.

"Thanks."

He pulls out my chair, and I sit, putting my purse on the round table that wobbles.

I don't notice the table much as my eyes are glued to his, and he asks what I want to drink.

"Vodka and cranberry?"

"Sure." Our waitress only has eyes for him as well, and she turns to get my drink.

He leans towards me, sending another waft of his cologne toward me, and my pussy clenches.

What is up with me? My body craves him like a pizza on a Friday night after a long day at work.

Fuck me, I'm beholding to this hunk, and I'm going to use him for the information I need. I want a career more than anything. I'm tired of kissing people's asses, doing the right thing, and living by everyone's rules and expectations. Tonight, I'm Rachel, the uncensored, lacking in makeup, and totally nude except for my clothing, Rachel.

I don't notice the thud of the drink being placed in front of me, but when Blake leans in to tell me something, I want to jump him right there.

What's running through my head right now? Well, let's just agree I'm going to hell with all my sinful thoughts.

5

BLAKE

Rachel takes a sip of her cocktail while the waitress lingers and tries to initiate a conversation with me. I don't have to watch her walk away to know she's swaying her hips with the hope that I will pass her my phone number before I leave.

If I were to pass her anything, it would be a note with, *"Only one woman has my attention tonight, and it's not you,"* written on it. Usually, women chase me, get what they want, and then get pissy when I don't follow up with a phone call the next day.

This comes with the territory of being the up-and-coming, hot offensive player who can score. Getting a lot of attention from women is great, but it wasn't always that way.

Being a bit of an introvert, my social skills aren't the best. It takes me a minute to warm up to a woman naturally. Over the years, I picked up bad words, new ways to diss someone's mother, and other feats easily because I mostly hang out with the guys. The team is my family. Women I dated never became embedded in our tight circle.

I was only interested in hockey, video games, and skate

nights when I was younger. I stayed home playing video games and trash-talking on the phone with my friends. By the time I got to college, girls started to notice me, and it hasn't stopped.

Life was simple when I wasn't around so many people. I'm still not comfortable in large crowds. I hate having to pose for pictures. Maybe I'm camera shy because I didn't have a mom around to take photos of me. I don't have any traditional first-day-of-school pictures like the other kids. Dad has some of me with my championship trophies.

To this day, my favorite place to be is on the ice. As a result, I'm more at home in skates than I am in my boots. But I love my boots and my country roots.

I watch Rachel sip her drink, look around the bar, and survey the landscape. At her age, the bar scene is nothing new, and I hoped she'd be in her element and want to shine because she's so pretty.

But as the seconds tick by, I can tell she avoids meeting my eyes that something has happened to her. She looks like a flight risk because she's not fully sitting in her chair, and her feet are pointed toward me, but she's eyeing the door. I'm curious about what happened in Quebec to make her leave abruptly.

Sharing a locker room with my teammates, we learn each other's quirks, strengths, and weaknesses. Recently, I learned my weakness is getting into relationships quickly. I'm bowing out a year later because I know it won't work out. Before I moved here, I decided to take time off for myself. I want to invest time in learning who I am to make better decisions.

Then I remind myself Rachel is my rebound girl, nothing else. I know better than to date the neighbor. I shouldn't even be out with her, but after her embarrassing wardrobe malfunction and how she was cool about it, she won points with me.

It takes balls to go outside wearing slippers the size of clown shoes and a bathrobe fit for. . . well, fit for someone of my stature. Most girls would have run inside the minute they saw me.

She has the kind of tenacity it takes to hang out around jocks. Hockey players are all about teasing each other and giving each other shit. Now, I envision her walking around my place wearing only my t-shirt. We'll start with the one I'm wearing.

I looked around to see if Rachel was here when I arrived at the bar. I'm a guy, and I know it's ridiculous even to contemplate the fact she could arrive before me. I know how much time women need to get ready, and it's closer to waiting for the end of time than the seven days to create the Earth.

I snagged a table where I could watch the door, and I ordered a beer. Two minutes later, she waltzes in, and the number of heads turning to see her creates a brisk wind.

She earns extra points for not taking all night to get here. Women who are always late are high maintenance, and I had enough of that with my ex. She was a model. Every time she stepped out of the house, it was newsworthy.

I'm surprised Rachel showed up because she seemed reluctant when I suggested we meet. I lean back in the chair and stretch out my long legs before I stand up and head her way. What happened to you, Rachel? Are you running away from something or someone in Quebec?

I tell myself none of it matters as I take her fitted blouse. She's dressed conservatively. She's hiding her perfectly round breasts I received a glimpse of earlier. I imagine what it would be like running my hands over them. I'm sure they are firm, and her skin would be silky. I approach her and switch my thoughts off of her body. I'd be happy if my hard cock doesn't greet her first. I can be a jerk, but that would be downright rude.

She's piqued my curiosity, but if I learn everything about her, this is no longer the casual hookup I've promised myself it would be.

I walked to her and called her name before I realized one of us needed to break the ice, so I go first. "Thanks for coming."

First dates are usually a game of twenty-one questions. Most girls know all about me going into the date, but they still ask plenty of silly questions.

"Thank you for getting me out of the house." She manages a half smile.

"You looked like you needed rescuing—no one our age should spend a weekend night in a bathrobe and slippers."

She chuckles. "True." She quickly takes me in with her unusual blue eyes and looks away.

Another woman in tight pants and a low-cut shirt, showing more cleavage than necessary, walks by, giving me the eye, and it lasts so long that Rachel notices.

"Do you know her?"

"Oh," I brush it off, "no."

"Mm," she replies, but she's no fool. I'm afraid she might be on to me. Tonight, I'm Blake, a country boy in a country bar.

"I have a table. Follow me," I say, and we end up drinking our first drink together, sitting on hardwood chairs.

The band plays a familiar tune, filling the dance floor.

"You dance?"

"Some, but I don't know if I can do that." She nods to the line dancers kicking their feet with the Boot Scootin' Boogie song.

"Oh, you could do it, no problem." I stand, putting my hand out.

She takes it; if I had a tail, it would wag. Down boy! I remind myself this is a night to have fun without attachments. I'm Blake—the unattached, newly single guy only looking for a fun night. Hell, I should print out business cards with that on them.

I reach for her hand and find hers warm as it slips into mine. We make our way onto the worn wood floor and join a line of people already dancing. She watches my feet and mimics my moves. I'm convinced everything she does is adorable. Before I know it, she's grinning ear to ear, and so am I.

The locals are better at this, having danced to these choreographed moves longer for years. To their credit, there's probably not much else to do for fun as we're out of the city lights.

When the song ends, Rachel is a bit breathless but smiles and accepts another drink when I order another round.

"That was a workout," she says, lifting the hair off her neck to cool down.

I'm mesmerized by her piercing blue eyes that sparkle even in this dim lighting. I imagine her hair is soft if I were to run my fingers through it.

The drinks I ordered finally arrived, and the waitress winked at me when I thanked her. I slip her money for the drinks and a nice tip. I avert my eyes when I notice she recognizes me. No response is needed.

"I'm so thirsty." Rachel lifts her mixed drink and drains it.

I lift my beer and do the same, not taking my eyes off hers.

"What are you thinking?" She asks, her hand rests on the empty glass.

"That you're beautiful," I answer, taking her hand. We hold hands at the table until my cock is like a steel rod in my tight designer jeans. I can't sit a minute longer.

I stand. She follows suit. I glance around as the music fades into the background. Instead of music, I hear my heart pounding in my ears. Each second makes it beat faster. This is fun. I like being spontaneous.

After seeing her move on the dance floor, I want to score a different kind of workout. I've been here enough times to know there's a storeroom in the back.

Standing toe to toe, we're so close the heat radiates between us. It's time to make my move. Our lips meet, and it's like an explosion in my head. My body is on fire. I have to have her. The chemistry between us is overpowering. She's so hot I want to take her right here. Common sense prevails, and I know I need to take this somewhere more private.

I lead her to the storeroom. I try the door, and as luck would have it, it's unlocked. We slip inside, and I lock it behind us. I pull her into an embrace, and our hands are all over each other, our lips searching, sucking, and nipping each other in a whirlwind of pure lust. I pick her up and pin her against the concrete wall.

Wrapping her legs around my waist, she pushes herself up on me as I run kisses down her neck while popping the buttons off her blouse to pull her bra down and grab a handful of the perfect breasts I fantasized about earlier. I can't wait a second longer as I lean down and kiss her smooth, untanned skin.

My cock swells in my pants as I take her nipple in my mouth. I suck on it, which makes her nipple harder than it was a second ago. A moan of pleasure escapes her lips. Lips I left swollen with the intensity of our first make-out session.

I strip off my shirt and relax, letting her soft fingertips

explore my chest, then move to my hard biceps, going over them gently, meticulously feeling every muscle as they quiver under her touch.

I continue to nip at her nipple while unbuttoning her jeans and working my hand down. I find her lacy panties and push them to the side. It's a tight fit, but I manage to get two fingers in her and move them methodically, slipping them in and out. I watch her face until her eyes close, and her head rolls back, limp with pleasure.

I hit my mark because it sparks a chain reaction whereby her manicured nails dig into my skin. A guttural moan leaves her lips. For a brief moment, I fear she may pass out as she becomes breathless, but then her nails turn into bear claws as I inch my fingers deeper into her. I'm surprised by the strength in her small hands. It's fucking hot. And I love pain.

I'm tough. I've been body-checked up against the boards, but this is the most enjoyable contact I've had with a wall outside the rink.

When she reaches down and unzips my pants, I know she wants it as bad as I do. Good thing I went commando tonight. My cock is constricted, and my balls hurt with an ache to fill her. She releases my throbbing cock from his cramped cage, and he springs out like a boom on a repo truck, hard as steel. My blood is pumping hard, and my cocks throbbing vein is evident. Its slight curve is perfect for reaching the G-spot that women crave.

I like her enthusiasm as she strokes my cock with her hand, then grabs harder as she bites into my shoulder, driven by excitement and desire. It's a turn-on to pursue a woman for a change. I smile against her neck and nip at her earlobe, and I struggle to undo the rest of the zipper on her jeans and tug them down far enough to make entering her with my giant cock a possibility.

I've been with my share of women, but Rachel is different. Tasting her sweetness is more than I need to make me want to bury my cock in her; it becomes my will to live. I tug her panties down, and with my feet firmly planted on the concrete floor, I thrust my engorged cock into her rather hard. She gasps, and her nails dig into me to brace herself. I thrust into her time and time again. Feeling her warm, tight pussy, I moan as she withers against me.

Light from the bar filters in under the door. The music from the band reverberates through the wall. Our body heat makes the room as hot as a sauna.

"Fuck me," she cries out as she rakes her nails over my back and grabs me tight, clinching my muscles in her hands. I'm digging the pain; keeping her on the wall is not a problem. My body is built for this.

I grab a fistful of her long blonde hair and pull it hard as her pussy grips my throbbing cock, and we both explode at the same time and crumple against each other. After catching my breath, I let her down slowly until her feet touched the floor, but we held onto each other, unable to stand on our own.

My calves are cramping from the workout, and she has tiny beads of sweat on her face.

"I'm sorry about your blouse," I say as she pulls it closed over her ample boobs.

"Sorry about biting you."

"I liked—"

A knock on the door interrupts our moment, and we're busted.

I pull up my jeans and zip them as she straightens and checks to ensure her phone is still in her back pocket. I'm surprised it's in one piece.

"Fuck." My eyes quickly take in the look of panic in hers. I've done shit like this before, but I can't be caught doing it now. The press would have a field day, and management would crucify me.

"Shit," she mumbles as her panicked face turns to mine. "Let's make a run for it?"

"Sure," I agree. "Sounds good to me," I reply, pulling my keys out.

"Who's in there? Unlock the door. We need more wine," the voice from the hallway speaks.

"Coming out," I reply, and as soon as I unlock the door, I throw it wide open as we bolt out towards the red box with the word Exit that hangs over the door that has "Fire Escape Only" clearly marked on the push bar.

Fuck me. It's going to be noisy.

Alarms go off as we cross the threshold into the night's cold air. She keeps up with me as I sprint across the parking lot. I'm scared shitless of tonight's events ending up on the news, but we're both giggling as we slide into my Charger, and I tear out of the parking lot.

I hope they don't have any video cameras behind the building recording our escape. Either way, she was worth it. That was officially my rebound fuck, and it was like a scene out of a movie. Only, it's my life, and the freedom fits me like a glove.

6

RACHEL

Blake grabs my hand and yells, "Come with me."

We run through the parking lot until he stops at an orange sports car. My heart is racing as we open the doors simultaneously and jump in.

"What is this?" I ask, having never been in a sports car like this before. This is definitely too expensive to keep with the cost of taxes and gas in Canada. Not many can afford it unless you're a movie star or a pro hockey player. That's why every boy playing hockey wants to go pro: hockey, girls, and cars.

Who can blame them?

"It's a Dodge Charger. Now buckle up," Blake shouts quickly before peeling out of the parking lot.

I put on my seatbelt like I'm in an American action flick, bracing for the ride of my life, high on adrenaline before I turn around in my seat to see if anyone is following us. "Looks like we're in the clear."

"Great. Wanna go for a ride?"

"Sure." What else was I planning to do besides go home and dream about him? That session in the storeroom was fucking hot as hell. I'll never look at a storage room quite the same again.

He floors it, and we pull onto a highway for a bit and then off into the countryside with its rolling hills and curves. We fly across an old bridge, and I'm worried we might hit a moose or deer on these dark country roads. It's risky, and I'm scared shitless, but dammit, it's exhilarating.

We're flying down a road when he hits a dip in the pavement that makes the car sink, and my tummy is tickled, and I let out a 'hell yeah!'

He laughs and throws me a grin that pulls at my heart-strings. He's loving this as much as I am. The car makes a donut as he turns around in a parking lot covered with gravel. We drift more than he expected, but his expert driving has us missing an old concrete milk house that used to keep milk and butter cool.

"Fuck," I scream, coming face to face with my mortality before being jerked away. I'm on a roller coaster that just changed course without warning.

"I got it," he assures me as he downshifts and gets us back on the road headed for town.

"It's getting late, and I have work tomorrow," I say.

"I'll swing by the bar, and if the coast is clear, you can get your car."

"Thanks." I'm having fun, but I also have obligations and an early alarm set.

He pulls into the lighted parking lot, and I point to my car. He parks next to it and gets out to open my door.

Leaning against my car, it dawns on me I had more fun in the last few hours than I've had in years. "Thanks for dragging me out tonight."

"No charge for breaking and entering, setting off emergency exit alarms, and exceeding the speed limit," he jokes.

I laugh. He's cocky, but his mad driving skills saved me from a near-death experience with a milk house, so I cut him some slack.

Things feel out of my control, yet I'm truly alive for the first time in my life.

The attraction I have for him is paralyzing.

He leans in, kissing my lips softly, then adding some tongue before pulling away. "Thanks for a great night. Get home safely."

"Will do," I say as I fumble with the key fob. I'm clumsy with foreign gadgets. I press the right button, and my door locks and unlocks. It's the fob, I tell myself. It's not because he could easily be my next addiction. Once I get into the car, I look in my rearview mirror and notice him idling in his vehicle, ensuring I'm safely in mine before he floors it out of the parking lot.

I, however, sit with my hands on the steering wheel. I'm unsure of my next move. The word rattled doesn't come close to how I feel. Tonight was an intense and exciting experience. I don't know if it qualifies as a date.

It's getting late. I gaze at the full moon. I can't sit here all night, so I cautiously exited the parking lot. After touching the home button on the navigation system, I'm confident I'm heading back to my brother's place.

Without thinking about directions, I get lost in remembering what went down tonight. Christ, that was the hottest sex I've ever had. I want more, but it's never going to happen. Tonight was like catching lightning in a bottle. He lives next door, and the least he can do is not parade his one-nighters past my front door.

When I pull into my driveway, I notice no light emanating from his house. Did he stay out to party at another bar? With Callie's car safely parked in the garage, I lock it with my fingertip. I enter the house through the white wood door ahead of me. I place my purse on the granite countertop and head toward my room.

I undress and take my second shower of the day. It's with mixed blessings that I use the all-natural soap in the cubby. I'd love to sleep with the scent of him on my body. I step out, grab a blue monogrammed towel, and dry myself. Keeping the smell of his cologne mixed with sex will only prolong my misery when he pretends he doesn't know me tomorrow. I predict tonight is a one-and-done situation because most relationships start slowly, not shooting out of a cannon.

I found my brother's t-shirt sitting in the dryer earlier today. I pull it on for comfort because I'm overcome with anxiety. I'm alone in the States until my brother returns. I walk to the kitchen and drink a glass of water before I slide into bed. I smile when I remember tonight's Bonnie and Clyde-style getaway, minus the bullets. I pull my laptop from the nightstand, open it, and begin typing.

I'm in the zone; before I know it, it's past one in the morning, and I have to get up for work in a few hours. I close my magical writing machine and push it aside for the night. I check my phone, making sure the alarm is set. I'm optimistic my first day at the new job tomorrow will go off without a hitch; I slide under the covers. Exhausted and a bit bruised, I drift off to sleep thinking about Blake and all those muscles, but my favorite one was between my legs.

My phone alarm dings and dings until I finally shut it off. Crap, today is like the first day of school, and that's just ridiculous, as I'm an adult. Treating the first day of any new experience with an ounce of trepidation is healthy. It's the fear of the unknown. Tomorrow should be better, but first, I have to tackle today.

What should I wear to a job that requires me to cater to and kiss the ass of some rich, spoiled jerk while pretending I like it?

Knee pads?

I pick a conservative midi dress. The blue color makes my eyes appear darker, and that's how I like it. Still sleepy from my late night, I head to the kitchen and make coffee with the help of the Keurig machine.

The caffeine will perk me up, but I need makeup to help me look awake, so I bring the cup of hot coffee with me into the bathroom. I can do my makeup better than most professional makeup artists, and I'm done in less than ten minutes. If I had a superpower, it would be the tagline "making the ordinary look extraordinary." Because, like magic, it's all an illusion. I'm not that pretty.

Wearing my most comfortable pumps, I make another cup of coffee for the road. I grab the car key, my purse, and my phone. I get in the car, check my lipstick, and make sure the arena is on the phone's app before I start my drive to the arena. I have no clue what to do with a modern car. It scares me when it talks to me. It dings if my seatbelt isn't on. The safety features are insane and impractical. Apparently, I child-proofed myself. The issues are too numerous to count for a person used to mass transit.

I hope my new boss isn't an asshole. My brother, Alexandre, used to be the poster child for asshole behavior, so my expectations are at rock bottom. I park in the next to empty parking lot and check in with security at the glass doors of the main entrance. I ask a secretary for directions to the conference room. Making my way down the empty, carpeted halls, I pass by Callie's office. The team is still in what is called the off-season, and it's also known as the wedding season. I'm not surprised it's quiet.

My brother knows someone at an employment agency who takes vetted applicants, like me, and matches them with professional athletes to be their assistants. They weed out the stalkers and bunny boilers. Naturally, I assume I will be following around some bigwig at the arena, doing secretarial stuff or personal shopping. Won't that be fun?

The double doors to the conference room are closed, and when I open them, I find one person sitting at the enormous table—

Blake.

"Oh, wow, are you here for the job, too?" I ask, thinking I was a shoo-in, but maybe this is a follow-up interview.

He looks dashing in a white Henley shirt and black jeans as he leans back in the office chair and runs his long fingers through his hair.

"Job?" He chuckles, looking more and more like the cat that ate the canary. I look for scratch marks on his arms, and after seeing none, I fear that I dreamed the whole thing last night.

How did he get in here? Does he know my brother and his wife? I want him to stop grinning and start talking, but being tongue-tied, all I can ask is, "What?"

"Are you here for a personal assistant job?" He stands and approaches me as if we've never met.

"Yeah, how'd you know that?"

He extends his hand. "Hi, I'm Blake Gibson. I play offense for the Maulers. You'll be working for me."

Fuck me, and all that is holy.

BLAKE

I could not have been more surprised to see Rachel than if a stripper had walked in, dropped to her knees, and blown me in front of my mother.

I never imagined my new neighbor would be my new assistant.

"Um," she fumbles. "We can't work together."

"Sure we can. Why not?" I ask as she walks closer to me. This is our first meeting as working adults, and she still takes my breath away. Truthfully, I want to fuck her again.

"I'm sure there is a conflict-of-interest clause somewhere."

"How is there a conflict? We hooked up before we met professionally," I protest. "Have a seat." I gesture to the chair near me.

Smoothing her pretty blue dress under her sweet ass, she sits in an office chair as far away from me as possible yet remaining in the room. I try not to be offended, but with her at the opposite end of the conference table, this feels more like the standoff at the O.K. Corral than a working relationship.

"Um, can we pretend last night never happened?" Her meek voice barely reaches me.

"Sure, but what's the fun in that? Seems to me it was very memorable." I can't hide the smirk on my face as I lean back in the padded business chair, feeling comfortable in my fitted street clothes and matching sneakers.

She doesn't look at all like she did last night. A few hours ago, she was dressed for a country bar, but now, she's all business with her flawless makeup. I'll say she's gonna fit right in with the wives and girlfriends of the players, or as we commonly call them, the WAGS.

"That was then, this is now," she says, making her point. "When I say now, I mean this is a 'working environment' where the boss doesn't have sex with the employee. In other words, we can't let that happen again." She sends me a defiant glare, but I can tell last night is playing through her head by the soft and vulnerable look in her eyes.

Her long, wavy hair is in an updo, showing off her long, slender neck, the way professional ballerinas would wear it.

A few tendrils of hair fall around her delicate face. I fight the impulse to kiss her mouth and touch her body. Her being here turns me inside out, so I can't let her talk me out of this. The attraction between us can't be denied. Our hormones are symbiotic, blending together like two flames dancing. Flames are ignited without the need for an accelerant or a match.

I barely slept last night because I couldn't stop thinking of her, which is why I'm so tired now.

"Even if I find you irresistible and the night is worth repeating?"

"Yes. I mean, no," she replies. "Find someone else." She fidgets with the purse in her lap, opening and closing the clasp, and her eyes fall to my chest.

Nervous, turned on, and defensive are the vibes I'm

detecting. Someone hurt her. But who? Is she hiding from an ex back in Canada?

"What if I don't want anyone else?" It's fun making her squirm as she shifts in her chair.

"Human Resources will have something to say about that." She shifts, sitting taller in her chair as if it will give her words more weight, but she's bluffing. I can read body language. I'm a hockey player; there is no way she's faking me out. I'm on offense. She's painfully on defense. There's no way she's running away from this. I can tell she wants me. Why else would she want to bail on the job so quickly?

"That's all taken care of. Do you think I'd be with any woman without a non-disclosure agreement today? The company that hired you should have emailed it."

"Hm, it seems like you're putting the cart before the horse or whatever that saying is. Let's agree that the horse has left the stable. I could spill everything to the press," she says, but her voice lacks conviction.

"You're bluffing," I say. If she were going to do that, it would be after we broke up, out of spite. But I don't think she's capable of being spiteful.

I bring my chair closer to her and lean on the table to hear what she comes up with next.

"No NDA for last night, nothing stopping me." She says the words flippantly. I don't think she's capable of not caring about herself or me.

"You don't have it in you," I push.

"Oh, don't I?" Her voice grows louder with each word, and she stares me down.

"Face it; you wanted me as much as I wanted you."

Silence. Game, set, match. Or rather, tripped, pinned, and body-checked.

I can't stop the smirk that pulls at the corners of my mouth.

"Oh, stop gloating."

"What?" I'm feigning innocence.

"Let's get to work," she suggests.

"Work it is." I stand. "Let's go to the training room. It should be empty. Having never been here, I assume you'd like a personal tour."

As we walk down the hall, we're within inches of each other. My cock thickens, and I'm glad there's room in my loose-fitting pants to conceal my desire.

Except for the bathrooms and the stairwells, this building is full of security cameras. It's so tempting to pull her into any one of these stairwells and bang her like last night, and just as exciting. I want to get to know every inch of her body, but that requires time and a softer playing field.

There are so many things I'd love to do to her again, only better and more of it. She enjoyed last night, but now, it seems she finds safety in keeping her distance, and we're starting over on a professional foot. We'll see how long she can stick to that.

"I'll take you around the facility, then give you a list of stuff to follow up on for me. I'm doing a huge charity golfing event in a few days," I say, filling her in as I lead the way down the player's corridor.

"Really, where is it?"

"The Turks and Caicos area, St. Bart's to be exact. I will email you the information. Book a bungalow with two rooms so that I can use the private swimming pool in between them. You'll stay in one room, and I'll stay in the other. The bungalows are over the water and so secluded it will feel like we're on our own island. You'll love it."

"I'm going with you? Surely that's overkill," she jests,

practically running to keep up with my long legs and fast pace.

If she thinks her little pushback will intimidate me, she doesn't know me. For instance, I always get what I want. If not, I wouldn't be in the NHL.

"By the way, your last name is Holloway. Is your brother Alexandre Holloway?"

I make it sound like nothing, but sometimes dating sisters doesn't sit well with teammates. Sisters are typically put on pedestals on hallowed fucking ground. They're considered off-limits according to bro-code, but rules were made to be broken.

"Yes, I'm staying in his house. I was between jobs so he's helping me with this gig."

Shit.

I had no idea Alexandre even lived in the house next door, and I have no idea how this will play out. Last night was just a fling, a one-night escapade. So why don't I want to let her out of her contract? It would be safer for me, and I promised myself a year of freedom.

"Well, I need you to run interference if any women are stalking me. That means you can pretend to be my girlfriend. Just a head's up, I'm terrible with small details, like directions and remembering my hotel room number."

I look over just in time to see the expression on her face fade from a smile to a frown. I have no idea why. Her face looks like she has a question.

"What?" I stop walking, and so does she. She's not moving her lips.

"Nothing," she replies, but I can tell she's thinking. "Only I'm not so good at those things either."

I don't know if she's trying to find a way out of the situation, mitigate how much we have in common, or something else altogether.

We've known each other a hot minute.

I take that back. A few hot, steamy, volcanic minutes that left me wanting more. And the joy ride to nowhere, she loved that, too. I can't deny I showed off my mad racing skills.

Ashley never liked my driving. She liked to stay on the highway and stay within the speed limit. She liked to be in control of everything, and that included me. It started with us wearing color-coordinated clothing to every event and ended with her telling me how to style my hair and when to shave my beard. I don't mind looking good for my woman, but the micromanaging I can live without.

Rachel whips out her phone to take notes, I suspect. Watching her fingertips fly over the screen, I remember them raking over my back last night and leaving behind scratch marks I can still feel. Her passion is impressive.

We're close in age, but seeing her work that phone, yeah —she acts like a millennial, but I know she's a GenZ. Then it clicked, her resume said she was an influencer and is good with social media.

"By the way," I say, pulling open the door to the team's gym. "I need you to handle my personal social media stuff, too. You'll have a contact person with the team. They will ask for pictures. You'll need to book my photo shoots when we get back, and you need to know what content you can upload and all that good stuff. There are rules in the NHL."

I hear her say, "Okay," but she hasn't looked up from her phone.

Good thing I opened the glass door for her before she ran into it.

I stop just inside the door to our gym, and she almost bumps into me.

I patiently wait for her to look up.

"Holy shit," she says with her cute accent when she sees the room.

"Nice, huh?"

"Wow, is that one of those resistant current pools over there?"

"Yes, for rehabbing and then the hot tub for sore muscles and relaxing." I point to a corner of the room that's larger than most free-standing gyms.

"Holy fuck, a fireplace!" She rushes over to the floor-to-ceiling, double-sided stone fireplace.

She walks around it, touching the sides. I bet she could walk through it without hitting her head.

"This is insane." She checks inside it to make sure it's real.

"It's not your imagination." I chuckle. "It cost a few million. Upstairs are the treadmills and physical therapy rooms," I add as her eyes take in the spacious room around us.

"Come, the team locker room is this way," I say, opening the doors to a circular room.

A huge skylight in the ceiling allows sunlight to stream in, brightening the room and creating a spotlight on the team logo, the blue and purple colored moose.

"Oh my God," she exclaims, absorbing the shock and awe of the pampered world I live in.

"No wonder your homes are gorgeous. I mean, who wants to go home to a crappy apartment after experiencing this?"

I can't help but laugh. It's good to know she appreciates the finer things in life and knows she's not entitled to them.

"No." Her face lights up. Clearly, the tour has worked its magic. It's no surprise how hockey players get laid so quickly.

"Kind of exciting, huh?" I can't help myself. I'd love to

show her the sauna and spend the rest of the day having hot, slippery sex in there.

God, I'm the devil incarnate. Will I ever stop thinking with my dick?

I lose interest in most women by now, but with Rachel, it feels different. She intrigues me. I don't just want to fuck her —I want to get to know her.

"This place is amazing. Working here might not be so bad after all," she thinks aloud.

"So, I take it you'll take the job?"

8

———

RACHEL

Dumbfounded doesn't even begin to describe my facial expression when Blake introduced himself as my BOSS.

Fuck. What do I do now? I can't text Charlotte. She's gonna think I'm a complete idiot. This is a menial job; totally no way I can fuck it up. There must be tons of candidates who would love to follow a hunk like him around all day.

It was one hot, steamy hookup, no strings, and now it's confirmed—there can never be anything serious between us. My heart skips a beat as I remind myself he's off-limits. I'm disappointed on so many levels, one of which is that I didn't get my fill of him. He could easily become my most decadent and dangerous addiction. Besides, he's the hotness that burned into my keyboard when I wrote about our sex against the storage room wall last night.

Knowing he exists, and after having the most incredible sex ever—and in public (sort of)—it has left me with quite the dilemma. To be around him, knowing that I can't touch him, is going to make my life a living hell. I would never know what I'm missing if I had never sampled what he's serving. It's like eating that first potato chip and wanting more and eating them until the bag is empty. And I want more of…. Blake.

My body yearns for his touch and cock to fill me up again. I wish I had a shirt that reminds me of him to sleep with because I'd love to sleep in it. Standing this close to him, I secretly inhale his cologne and recall last night when that scent mingled with the heat of our bodies as my hands clenched and dug into his hard biceps.

Fuck, fuck, fuck.

My bad luck is worse than a herd of black cats who stalk me so that they can cross my path at every turn and screw up my life.

"Yes, I'll sign the forms and get up to speed on my emails and travel plans."

Once again, I find myself powerless over my destiny. I'm his employee, and I need this job.

"Great." He turns to shake my hand.

I give him mine, and we have a deal.

I just made a deal with the handsome devil, and I'm going to hell from the thoughts running through my mind as his touch gives me electrifying tingles that run up my arm and down to my warm pussy.

My brother gifted me this job. Of course, I can't say no. None of us could have predicted me being in the crosshairs between this incredibly sexy man, my job, and my brother. Last night, I didn't see him naked, but I did get more than my share of his incredible dick. And having his body pushed up against my chest so hard, my boobs are still sore.

As we return to the conference room, I get a video call from my parents. I can't face my parents, so I text them I'm fine. It's a lie, but I can't burden them with another chapter of mishaps in my life story that resembles a Christmas tree—

y'know how those strings of lights get so tangled up they are impossible to use?

My parents didn't understand my creative side and never knew what to do with me growing up. I was all over the map, chasing every shiny object to see where I fit in. And as much as I tried to escape my creative tendencies, I loved getting lost in them, especially books.

I'm not glued together like my brother. Creative types have to work to be organized, in my opinion. On the other hand, Alexandre had the structure, dedication, and drive to achieve his goals. It didn't hurt he did something our parents could participate in, unlike writing books, which is a solo mission. So, I spent most of my time in my head, putting down my thoughts.

Alexandre had our parents on the hook with every turn of his skates. They were there for him as he worked his way up to the pros. And I never fit in anywhere. Sure, I'd do well with a job, then I'd get waylaid repeatedly by something strange and lose my job.

I concluded that structured jobs just weren't for me. Then, my makeup videos took off, and the carpet was pulled out from under my feet. Failure is not an option when my brother stuck his neck out for me. I can't let him down and have Mom and Dad worry about me.

On top of the pressure to succeed, I know my brother pulled strings to get this gig for me. I can't let Alexandre down or compromise the family's good reputation back home any more than I already have. I'll suck it up for the greater good and work with Blake, which means I may never have this hockey hottie again.

"Okay, well, I'll send you those emails. But get on it. I might have a confirmation number for the hotel. So, just follow up." He walks to the doors that magically open for us, and I follow him back to the main arena.

"Sure. I'll get right on it. So that's it then?"

"Here, put your number in," he hands me his phone, "this way, I can text you as things come up. And email, too. I'm sure it's on your employment forms, but this is easier."

I take his phone, making sure our hands don't touch. Fornicating on the steps to the arena would leave some strange marks on both of us. Hell, I'm still recovering from last night.

I didn't have to try every position and location in one day, but the wall in the storeroom was a great start. Unfortunately, he's so off-limits I might as well live in another country—as in off the map.

However, I'd still choose to be here so I can secretly savor our hot fling and see what I can learn from him. I could make great contacts that could put me on my feet again now that I've had a glimpse of the athlete's world.

I need to Google Blake's bio when I get home. He has all my deets, but I know nothing about him.

I type my number into his phone and hand it back without batting an eye.

"Are you sure you want me for this job? I'm sure you can get a replacement," I suggest.

I hope it's not obvious that I'm sizing him up because he's got that effect on me. He's out of my league. Guys like him date actresses and models if they're not dating their high school sweethearts.

And, as Blake pointed out, he's got people all figured out. What does he think about me?

"You'll do." He throws a grin my way as we walk down the rest of the steps and toward the parking lot.

"I'll get that information over to you. Make sure you

follow up with the travel agency and get the airlines booked and all that," he commands like I'm a juvenile who needs directions on basic tasks.

As long as I don't have to cook, this is doable. I'll pretend the hot neighbor is still a stranger. I'm sure I can do that.

Right, and unicorns are real.

I'm chastising myself for going out last night. One night of fun, and it's another tricky situation for me. I'll never be able to forget the hot storeroom sex at the bar and the joy ride that followed. I chuckle. Actually, there were two joy rides, but only one required my jeans to be around my ankles and my panties to be shoved aside.

I did get a great start for the sex scene in my book, but one sex scene isn't enough. And it wasn't even conventual sex. Shit. I need more sex. However, sleeping around with the players like a puck bunny isn't going to look professional and will get me fired, an embarrassment I can live without.

I'm not one to jump from one guy to the next. Charlotte and I differ when it comes to when and where sex happens with men. Being single is not all it's cracked up to be. To find a guy with the same degree of chemistry I have with Blake may take a lifetime.

I'd love to find a dependable guy who has my back and understands my career. Am I asking too much for a man to support my career as I support them in theirs? And how will I know they are honest and trustworthy?

I get in Callie's car to go to the grocery store, but I can't stop my mind from reliving the memories of last night, the ones that give me hope I'm worthy of a good man with a cock to drill me in public places. Knowing we could have been caught made everything more exciting. I've heard about couples that get off on doing it in public places and how the thrill of being caught is a rush that makes the sex more intense.

I'm sure that's all I'm experiencing. That, and he's a good-looking jock who took an interest in me for two minutes.

Who wouldn't want the thrill of a high-speed car ride, the drifting he did . . . that only happens in the movies. The maneuver made the bottom of my stomach sink, proving it isn't my overactive imagination. I smile; maybe I'm an adrenaline junky like my brother.

The sun is bright, the sky is clear, and it's a perfect summer day as I pull into the local grocery store. Thankfully, my sweet brother left me money for food. Right now, I must get settled in my new profession as an assistant and stick to the script.

Because until I become a best-selling author, I'm stuck. Well, it's either that or wait until the situation at home blows over. I don't see that happening unless my social media accounts have a rebirth that would rival that of Jesus. Until then, I'm shit out of luck.

I enter Hanny's Supermarket and grab a cart. It's a large store, but they don't build grocery stores on every corner around here. With only one store in this elite suburban town, avoiding someone would be difficult, should that ever be necessary.

I peruse the beer and wine section, totally intent on grabbing a bottle of red, and I am about drop the bottle in my hand into the cart when I notice hard liquor on the shelf. Never have I ever experienced that. Maybe it's giving me a subtle message that Maniacs might drink to survive the winters. Or. . .loneliness.

Shit, it gets cold in Canada, too, but hard alcohol is in a different store. I chuckle. Maybe living here isn't so bad. I grab a second bottle of wine, hedging my bets since I'll be home alone with my vibrator and old movies with Zac Effron in them. I throw some frozen meals in the cart along with a pre-made salad so I feel better about eating the stuff I know is filled with chemicals and sodium. Come to think of it; those Hot Pockets look so effing good, gotta have some.

Crap, I will gain five pounds unless I start day drinking and stop eating. I'll work mostly from home. Who would know? Dressed in my sweat outfit in pale pink. . .

Of course, I can't do that, but it sounds nice.

I manage to navigate self-checkout and drive home unscathed.

No sooner do I get inside and unload groceries than Charlotte calls.

"What's up, how did today go?"

"Great, and not so great." Holding the phone to my ear, I walk around the house and stop at the picture window to admire the beautiful maple trees out front.

I blink and see Blake jogging by. He's shirtless. I chuckle, so that's what his chest looks like, and I swear he's slowing down as he passes my window.

"What's funny?" Charlotte asks.

"Hmm. Turns out last night's fling is my new boss and a professional hockey player."

"You're shitting me. You can't be serious."

"Nope, it's true."

"You have the worst luck ever, Rachel. I'm sorry, that sounds bad. I support you, but that's worse than bad luck. So, no more hookups, I take it?"

"Nope, strictly professional. I did get some great material

for my book last night, though. He fucked my brains out against the wall in a storeroom at the bar."

"No shit. I haven't done that in years."

I chuckle; she's not kidding.

"Yup, I stepped outside of my comfort zone, and this is what happens. But I have a job, so that's good," I reply.

"Yes, it is. Things up here are the same."

In other words, my name is still in the crapper.

"Guess I should publish my book under a pen name," I suggest, and I'm not surprised when she agrees. Besides, celebrities are the only people who use their real names to sell books.

I'm supposed to be moving forward with my life, not regressing. But how could I have known one kiss with Blake would leave me yearning for him to fill my needy pussy. I'm learning she is one greedy bitch and betrays me when it comes to sex. Sex has suddenly become my elixir of life.

"I suggested Blake, being my brother's teammate, hire a different assistant, which went down in flames like the Hindenburg blimp."

"I bet. Maybe he wants another round."

"Trust me, I'm not in his league. I bet I was a quick scratch for his horny itch."

"Well, you got something out of the hookup, which is more than most." She reassures me that being a tramp for a night probably served me just as much, if not more than it did him.

Maybe it won't be so bad working for him. Besides, he can be my muse. No one needs to know that. It will be my secret.

"You should see the training facility. No wonder these guys all live in mini-mansions and drive cars like Blake's. I can see the appeal they offer hot chicks. They live the life of the rich and famous, and it can be a powerful aphrodisiac if a girl wants that life."

"I'm sure, but you're not a mooch. You'd rather earn it yourself, so keep writing and send me the chapters you have done so I can read about this hot jock."

"Will do. Gotta go get some work done."

"Bye."

I change into comfy leggings and an oversized tee and grab a bottle of water before sitting on my bed, just like I did in college, and pull my magical writing machine, Belle, to my lap.

First, I checked my email and found those that Blake sent. I take notes while reading them, make some calls, and book flights using Blake's credit card on file with his travel agent. I question myself on protocols, but I have no way of knowing if other assistants travel with their bosses.

Looks like we'll be flying out in a few days. That's cutting it close to training camp, mandatory training camp. I read through all his forwarded emails regarding practice times and set up a shared calendar for us.

Now I have to write another chapter.

Blake's my neighbor, and I have to see him again… and again. What happens when he starts bringing home puck bunnies? How is that going to make me feel?

Ugh. Stupid me. Charlotte should have saved me from my horny fuck fest.

How can I be near him when his presence sets off warning bells in my head, and my pussy is wet for another round? I've read about all these different places and positions to try, but I've never been adventuresome. Now, I'm chomping at the bit.

After an hour of sitting in bed, I'm a bit stiff, but I'm able to slide off the bed and make it to the bathroom. It must be a few strained muscles from riding a horse named Blake.

After I pee, I'm washing my hands, and my lower back sends a shot of pain like a lightning bolt. I lift my shirt to check my back in the large mirror over the bathroom sink and see that it's red from scraping the wall. Oh my!

My first sex injury. I'm so proud.

9

BLAKE

Just when I think the going gets easy, life becomes complicated. I can't pursue Rachel. She's my assistant, but I'd rather have her around me working than to not have her around at all, which would happen if I slipped up.

She sent all the paperwork to the agency and is doing a fantastic job. I've never had anyone work for me before, but my agent suggested I get a personal assistant, a personal chef, and a nutritionist now since I finally made it to the first line on the team and I'm making more money.

I'm stoked about being on the first line. Next, I'll have promotions that I'll get paid well for because my name recognition is going up, and that equates to endorsement money.

I'm young and don't want emotional entanglements. I have plenty of time to find the right girl. The fact that Rachel was so big into social media is a good reason to steer clear of her. I had that with Ashley, and I hated every minute of it.

The fact that she used me like a pimp for her career left me cold. Between that and my difficulty trusting women since Mom left, it created an environment I was desperate to escape. Dad raised me and Sam. Mom surfaced years later, but it's a relationship I'm not too keen on.

My phone rings. Rachel. I need a ringtone for her. I guess I will need to learn more about her to get that off my list of things to do.

"Hi, what's up?"

"I have a list of chefs that were recommended. I'll email it to you."

"Great. I'll look it over."

"Okay, I'll swing by later and drop off your dry-cleaning."

"You have the code, right?"

"Yeah, I just don't want to interrupt you."

"I'm not seeing anyone if that's what you mean." And I don't know why she would be thinking this if she wasn't the slightest bit interested in me.

"Okay, good talk. I updated your calendar with your workout times, and your training days, and all our trip information is confirmed."

"Great. Thank you." I'm digging this assistant taking care of the minutiae I'm not into.

"I have the information from the individual photo shoots for the new season. You'll need to be there tomorrow at 8 a.m."

"Great. Thank you."

"You're welcome. I'm heading out to get your suits now."

"Cool." I hang up.

After my morning run through the neighborhood, I showered but needed to get into the gym. Our coaches would be pissed if I didn't show up to training camp in anything but top form. Showing up with a beer belly or a "dad bod" is a no-no.

I'm cutting it close, going to the charity golfing event on St. Bart's. But it's for a charity that is close to my heart, and I have a private meet and greet I have to attend there. I can't let Hannah down.

I take a quick look in the mirror to make sure my hair is slicked back perfectly before Rachel arrives. I head to the kitchen for my mid-morning snack.

Like magic, Rachel appears minutes after I make a protein shake. She lets herself in, carrying numerous suits.

I look up and stifle a laugh as she struggles to walk. The long plastic reminds me of a long train on a wedding dress.

"Should I put these in your closet?"

"Here," I walk across the spatial home towards her. "I'll help."

She hands half the clothes to me, then struggles to rearrange what's left in her hands as the bags drag on the floor because she's not that tall.

I put my lips together to keep from smiling at how cute she looks under those clear plastic bags. It's obvious she's never done this before.

Her raspberry body lotion makes my nose twitch. I wish I had some fresh raspberries in my morning shake. But I'd rather eat her instead. We arrive in my bedroom, and, once inside the large room, the bed is inviting with a fluffy white duvet begging to be messed up with hot, passionate lovemaking.

All I can think of is how I'd love to rub some Fuck Sauce over her nipples and clit before licking her until she comes numerous times. The sexual tension makes the Richter scale look like a warmup compared to my planned main event. We are next to each other; it's almost impossible not to touch her. I begin to sweat for no reason.

"Closet is here." I open the double French doors to the large walk-in closet. It's a closet any woman would kill for because it even impressed me. Who wouldn't want built-in shelves and an island in the middle for accessories?

"Holy cow, your closet is even bigger than mine. . . I mean Alexandre's."

And here I hoped she was going to refer to the size of my dick, but sadly, she's sticking to the rules.

"Perks of the neighborhood. Actually, my agent found it for me. I took time off this summer and recently moved here myself. I was in Los Angeles with my girlfriend, but we broke up. You might have heard of her, Ashley Hamilton."

"Hmm, not sure." She places my clothes in the section clearly built for suits, and I help the hangers land on the wooden rod as she marvels at my footwear.

"My, you are country; what a boot collection."

"Yeah, I have to admit it's one of my weaknesses. Shoes, that is, well, I have a few weaknesses." She blushes and I'm beginning to feel like I need air.

Reaching up, I grab a pair of brown boots. "These are Lucchese boots, they are handmade. It's the only boot I wear unless I'm mucking the stalls."

"Mucking the stalls?"

"Yeah, y'know, when you clean out stalls the horses live in when they aren't outside."

"Oh, I've seen it in movies. It just sounds weird coming from you. You play hockey. What do you know of horses?"

The confusion is written on her face.

"I'm from Minnesota, farm country mostly."

"Yeah, I was raised in the 'burbs in Quebec, so that's lost on me. Makes sense why you love country music."

"Yeah—we didn't get to hear much music the other night." I can't help but grin at the memory.

"Nope." She smacks her lips at the end of the word, and it makes me feel cheap that I just hooked up with her when a girl like her should be wined and dined. That would have happened in hindsight, but we live in an imperfect world.

"Those are pretty boots." She reaches her petite handout and feels the leather. "Soft as butter."

My dick hardens, and I think how incredible it would feel if she were rubbing. . .

"They're amazing. You'll have to get a pair one day." I struggle to keep my voice from lifting like my dick in my pants as I put them back on the shelf.

Then I feel like an ass as they are not cheap.

"I hate to ask, but I know you didn't bring much with you, judging from your suitcases. Do you need some clothes for the trip?"

From the hesitation, I hope I didn't offend her.

"What kind of things?" she asks, only I see the terror on her face and assume she's low on money.

We make our way back to the kitchen. "Have a seat."

She sits on the leather bar stool as I drink my shake one gulp at a time. I'm not in a rush, and I purposely want to keep her here on business as long as possible.

"Um, things like a nice dress for a fundraiser. Most girls have cocktail dresses, and there is always a pool, happy hour, and a dinner with suits and ties. A silent auction goes on at that time. I'll golf in the morning, so you'll have time to use the spa, get a massage, whatever."

"That sounds great, but I don't have clothes like that. I can't afford it. It's a long story, but basically, the boyfriend I broke up with screwed me over big time."

Her eyes narrow, like she's ready to cry, and I'm not sure if I want to comfort her or fuck her. She looks vulnerable and fuckable at the same time, as if that's even possible. Either way, it's a turn on that has my dick hard as a frozen pond.

"My ex made me look like a hypocrite. He tanked my

social media accounts, and all my corporate sponsorships were pulled. That was my bread and butter. Now, I'm hoping I can pay my half of the rent in Quebec and still have enough to make the payments on my laptop."

I let out a slow whistle and feel the blood leave my cock as my brain switches gears.

Now I can understand her reluctance to go out with me and why she might not trust men. I knew there was a story. Everyone has one.

"Wow, I'd say you've been through the wringer."

"Tell me about it." She laughs a sweet, soft laugh, like the ripple of a gentle babbling brook in springtime, a laugh I could get used to.

"So, as your boss," I clarify this to make sure she doesn't take my next question wrong, "how long are you staying in town? I'd hate to lose you."

Shit, she just got here. She can't leave now.

I finish my shake and hold my breath.

"If things work out, my roomie, Charlotte, that's my BFF, will rent out my half of the place. It's expensive to live in the city. We'll have to see how the job goes." She tilts her head up and cocks her head to see me towering over her from the other side of the island counter. She raises her eyebrows as if she's saying the next move is mine.

"Every city is expensive, isn't it?" I joke. "But you have this job, isn't that enough?"

"It is for now. I have a side project I'm working on, but it's a long shot."

She's inferring without elaborating on her side project, and I am dying to know her side hustle.

In my mind, she'll share it with me when she's ready. In the meantime, I'll have to figure out how to get more information on this side project so I'll have an inkling of how much time we'll have together—work-wise.

"So, we're gearing up for the trip." I changed the subject.

"Yes." Her enthusiasm rings louder than my coach's whistle. "I've never traveled except to watch my brother play, and I've been dreaming of a tropical vacation for years. You're from Minnesota, you know what real winter is like. And you just arrives here from the LA Thunder."

"That I do" I nod in reference to her comment about winters. She's been doing her homework on me. I never told her what team I came from.

"Yeah, below freezing temps for three months. So, yeah, this trip to the island is a dream come true. I don't feel right going when you're paying the expenses, and I'm not doing much, really."

"Nonsense. I love the calendar you made for us. You keep me on track, and things will get busier when the season starts. I have many projects in the works."

"Really?"

"Hmm. I'll fill you in when it's a lock."

"Okay, and I imagine I'll be here in February because that's when Alexandre's baby is due."

"Really? I didn't know. Shotgun wedding? Alexandre and I didn't meet yet."

"Kinda, we came in for the proposal at Wyatt and Emily's wedding earlier this month, and Callie and Alexandre had a small wedding shortly after that; we stayed at a hotel. I returned home, and after all the crap with my ex happened, I came back. It's not all figured out yet. I'm a work in progress. No one has figured me out." Her voice drops, pulling at my heart. The heart that's beating faster than usual.

She's pretty beaten up by life, and I remember my youth filled with conditioning, training, stick handling, and so many road trips it's a blur. But Dad made it happen for me. It doesn't sound like she's ever had anyone to have her back aside from Charlotte.

"You like it here?"

"Oh, yes. It's been about a week, and I'm still getting the 'lay of the land,' as they say, eh?"

"Me too. And we need to get you some clothes so you'll fit in on the trip."

"I can't do that." She stares out the window, avoiding all eye contact, clearly uncomfortable.

"Sure, I'll drive you myself."

"I've seen the fashion magazines, after all, I worked with makeup, and I know the cost of designer things. I don't want to feel like I owe you." She moves her hand to the countertop and stands. "I can make do. But I should be going."

She turns to go, but I don't want her to leave.

"Look, I can set up an expense account for you. My accountant will take care of it. See, nothing crazy." I raise my hands up, palms slightly open, throwing myself on the sword here for her to accept.

"Um, I don't know. I do need them for the event, but. . ."

"Look, I don't wanna hear any more buts. Why don't we go to Bayside Boutique tomorrow? It will take a few days for your expense card to arrive, so I'll just lay it out for you."

"Grr, you're making this impossible for me to say no." She moves towards the door.

I smile. Good.

Having Alexandre as an older brother with his crazy schedule as a kid, she probably assumed a less important role in the family. This explains her surprised look when I shower her with compliments. I want her to actualize what life is like when she's in the spotlight. I want her to have nice things, and we're going to start with clothes for the charity event. It's a great excuse to give her a taste of my world; besides, she'll need designer items to fit in on the trip.

"I'll pick you up at ten. I'll be done with my pictures by then, and we'll shop and do lunch."

"Alright," she says with a hint of her French accent. Not only will her French come in handy at St. Bart's, but I've discovered accents turn me on.

I have no fucking clue how we're going to be in the same bungalow with a pool between us and not take advantage of the situation.

I'm so screwed.

10

RACHEL

Blake knocks on my door before ten as if it's a date or something. Dressed in skinny jeans and heels, I open the door.

"Hello." He greets me as I take a second to observe him in his Maulers polo and fitted jeans.

I threw on heels because every girl knows they lift our full, curvy butt, and the Maulers tee was a gift from my brother. It will make trying on clothes easier.

"Hi, ya, I just need to grab my purse. Come in." I back away from the door, watch his frame fill the doorway, and notice the boots he showed me yesterday click over the tile.

I don't know why some people pay hundreds of dollars for what I'd pick up online or something used for a few loonies in a Canadian secondhand store.

However, being with Blake makes anything worthwhile as long as I get to stare at his cute fucking ass cheeks in those dark denim jeans that look like they were painted on him.

What I wouldn't give to yank them off him. My pussy quivered from being so close to him yesterday, and now, I'm terrified to be alone with him in the bungalow on the island.

It's a tropical island and would be romantic with the right person.

Plus, I'm a sucker for a bubble butt, good cologne, and a pretty smile. It's funny that I never recall anyone outside of high school who remotely fits the bill. I guess I got into the habit of taking who picked me instead of choosing the guy I wanted and pursuing him.

But Blake will end up with a model or someone he's known forever—eventually.

"Take your time," Blake interjects as I reach into my purse, touch my ID, and pull out my lipstick. I quickly roll the red stain over my lips. I close the cylinder, drop it back inside, and zipper my purse before walking out the door.

The shopping plaza is decadent. Upscale stores greet me. Large lettering displays the designer names on the buildings. Blake lets an attendant park his sports car.

If I were pretty, I'd be his arm candy as he escorts me inside the first store. The carpet makes me feel like a princess in jeans.

But the kicker is Blake escorts me everywhere like we're a power couple. Now, I can understand what this must be like on a larger scale, like a red-carpet event. I need to enjoy today as I'm sure I'm the person who won't be with him when he meets the press or does photo ops.

No, I'm the Canadian who talks a bit funny and says too many 'eh's.' If this gig falls through, I could wind up back in Canada sooner than expected. Besides, no jock of star quality would want a dirty blonde-haired ex-influencer to be the mother of his little jock kiddies.

My brother is different in that he stepped outside of himself to let Carrie in, and the fact that they work in the same building didn't hurt—they love hockey. Their personalities work as they both want the same things.

I have no idea what Blake wants, but I'd like to know.

"Ah, here we go, you definitely need to be here," he opens a door for me it's as if I entered another world. Another beautifully decorated store with so many choices for dresses, jeans, and shoes all in place makes me dizzy.

"I have no idea where to begin." I can't help but grin like a kid on Christmas morning.

"We'll get help." He motions to a salesperson, asks her to assist us, and gives her a list that he rattles off quickly.

Whoa. That rolled off his tongue like it was rehearsed. Maybe he missed me this morning.

I quickly dismiss the idea as soon as it pops into my head. There is no way he'd ever think of me as someone to date. He's probably still texting his ex. Isn't that how it goes? I don't want to be his rebound. I tell myself this, but I'd be lucky to have him, period. But God, I want a redo of that hot, steamy night. If I don't get my itch scratched soon, my vibrator is going to melt down into a blob of silicone.

I can't erase our hot sex episode no matter how hard I try; he may have ruined me for all other men. If I had another job, I'd take it, but they aren't easy to come by in Maine, where it's still potato farms, commercial fishing, shipbuilding for the government, and guys with their butt cracks out that do the real back-breaking labor like welding and trucking.

"Hi, I'm Kelsey. I'll help you today. I understand you're going on a trip. We have everything you need. Follow me," the sales associate says.

Kelsey resembles an older Barbie doll who looks like she loves fashion as much as the top designers, judging from her coordinated jacket and skirt, white dress shirt, and black pumps.

I wonder if I need to dress like her when I'm in public with Blake, and maybe that's partly the reason for this shopping expedition. I don't measure up, but I'm such a glutton for punishment that I'd rather be around him than not be with him at all.

I try on clothes and trust Kelsey and Blake to make choices for me. I don't mind because I want to look my best. Besides, what do I know about being glamorous in a dress?

I'm the misfit. I live to be comfortable in my clothes when I'm not having to dress for work.

I return to the fitting room to try on another dress and look for the price tag. There isn't a price on it, only the size. It's one of 'those' shops. I make the decision to suck up my pride and let him treat me to a collection that will come in handy at the charity event. I rationalize this, telling myself I'll be able to wear everything a second time throughout the year. I imagine there will be numerous events these stellar, studly men attend. What if they win the Cup?

Kelsey gathers all the clothes that have made the cut on a clothes rack behind the register. She then places everything that hangs on a hanger in a huge cloth travel bag. These stores don't use clear plastic like a dry cleaner. *Interesting.*

I refrain from gasping at the total bill and try to wipe the surprise off my face. For now, this is my world, and I'm going to get lost in it because life has repeatedly proven to me that this won't last.

None of it. Not the sports car, the clothes, the trip to St. Bart's. It's as if I'm living a lie. This isn't me.

The clothes fit perfectly, and the tops for the jeans are made of cashmere, the silkiest, softest material I've ever laid my hands on. I'd love to prance around in it without a bra to feel its softness against my nipples and have it drape gingerly over my abs.

"Ready?" Blake asks as he carries the large bag for me.

"Sure. How do you get your equipment in this car?"He hangs my new wardrobe in the back of his sports car. Even I know this isn't a practical car.

"It's tricky, but it can be done." He opens the car door for me. "Let's eat."

We drive around the plaza, and there is one huge restaurant after another. George Clooney and Amal would take a boat ride to these types of places. We cruise by Camden Bay, and I see a restaurant with an outdoor seating area.

"You looked great in that black cocktail dress. The blue dress is stunning, too," Blake says as he keeps his eyes on the road.

"Thank you for helping. You've done too much." I glance at Blake as he drives, and then he glances at me. Is the seat heater on? I'm warm down there, and the sun coming through the window isn't helping my situation.

We share a smile, and time stops. The music on the stereo fades to black, and I'm lost in his smoldering eyes.

We get out, and a valet parks the car. I take comfort in the fact that we can work together, and after the first day, it hasn't been as awkward as I thought.

I fantasize about him as I drift off to sleep each night, and I wonder if that's healthy.

"The reviews on this place are great." He puts his hand on my back in a friendly manner, guiding me up the narrow walkway made of stones. It's one in the afternoon judging by the sports watch on my wrist. The place is packed, and every woman in the place stares at Blake, devouring him with their eyes as we're led to a table on the water.

"This is incredible." I sit in my chair as Blake sits beside me.

Hmm.

A waitress greets us; we both order iced tea as I peruse the menu, determined to find the least expensive item. Only the pages overwhelm me, and I love seafood.

"What would you like, Rachel? Calamari is good anywhere."

The teas are delivered to our table. I divert my attention by putting my straw in the glass and sip on the cold, home-brewed tea. Just in time, too, as my caffeine withdrawal is about to hit, and that won't be a pretty look. I need hydration and food after power shopping.

"You choose." It's always an easy response.

"I didn't take you as the kind of woman who wants all the decisions to be made for her," he teases with a twinkle of his gorgeous light blue eyes.

"Um." I put my drink down. "You're right, but there are times when it's refreshing not to make decisions all the time. It's hard running your own business. It's not just being good with makeup; I had to get followers and sponsors and learn how to market myself. It was brutal."

"I've never been there, so I'll take your word for it."

The waitress reappears, Blake orders appetizers, and we both order the fish plate with more sides than shoes in my closet.

"That wasn't too difficult," he surmises, drinking his tea.

"Blake, OMG." The voice is unknown to me, but I assume it's the woman coming to our table. She is roughly our age and is drop-dead gorgeous. A Louis Vuitton bag dangles from her arm, and she uses her other hand to push her sunglasses with a large G onto her head.

"Annie." Blake stands and kisses her cheek. "This is my new assistant, Rachel. She's Alexandre's sister from Canada."

"Nice to meet you." I shake her perfectly manicured hand, wondering what their relationship is.

"What have you been up to?" she asks Blake.

"Working out mostly."

"You never text me after our lunch. I was hoping I could show you around more," she said, flashing a smile that would melt the shine off a silver fork.

I'd say she was a cheerleader.

"You know, busy getting ready for training day, and I'll be out of town for a few days."

"Sounds fun. Well, I'll leave you to enjoy this beautiful day. I hope to see you soon."

"Sure thing," he replies and sits.

Annie waved to us both before rejoining an older woman in the distance who was waiting for her.

"Annie, huh?"

"Yeah, it's nothing. She's the coach's daughter. She just graduated. Her mother and I met at the community pool; she wanted us to meet as we're close in age."

"I bet the coach's daughter is a no-no." Pings of rivalry hit me when he said her name. I take comfort in knowing Annie's dating situation is more difficult than mine. Players see the coach's daughter as off-limits or a challenge.

I can't contain an outright grin as he shrugs his shoulders.

"You're right on that one. That's why I don't answer her texts." He smiles as he lifts his tea to his almost symmetrical lips. But I know from experience the bottom one is larger, as I've sucked on it profusely.

The appetizer arrives.

"So…" I reach for food to put on the tiny plate I find

heavy for something so small. "What was your breakup with Ashley like?"

"Oh, a girl arrives at our table, and now it's twenty-one questions on my love life?"

"I told you mine." I play defense.

"True. Okay, so she moved up the ranks with her modeling career. We both traveled a lot, and I wasn't feeling it. Little things started to bother me. I knew we weren't right of each other from the beginning, but we had some good times."

"That's too blah," I tease.

"That about sums up my thoughts on it, too." He furrows his eyebrows as if to say it's my turn for a great comeback.

"Ouch," is all I have in my tank. I'm stunned he's not still in love with his ex. "You can tell when you meet someone that they aren't right for you?"

"Pretty much, don't we all? I bet you knew with Joel."

"True." I succumb to his banter and logic, and now, the heavenly food is making its way to our table.

I'm surprised Blake takes such an interest in me, but maybe I'm an embarrassment to be around dressed as casually as I am for this ritzy place.

My salary isn't enough to afford the clothes that fit in with Blake's social circles. I wonder who named us personal assistants anyway. PA- personal assistant, does that mean I'm moving down in the world? I used to have my own business, and now I have no clue how long I'll be in Maine or where I'll be a few months from now.

I can't be a failure. I can't fuck up another job.

11

BLAKE

Rachel has no clue how beautiful she is. Even though I pretended to be uninvolved in her shopping, I did enjoy her youthful responses to the latest trendy fashions. Some stores have new collections that haven't hit mass distribution yet.

All it takes is for one famous person to be photographed wearing something from a new collection to make that designer an overnight success. The same could happen if I endorse a vodka brand. Name recognition goes a long, long way.

I've overindulged myself with half the day spent with Rachel, and the bits and pieces of her life are shaking out of her like leaves falling from the pre-winter winds. But she hasn't revealed her career plan with me—the 'long shot' as she puts it.

It was nice bumping into Annie, and the look on Rachel's face was priceless. I saw she was jealous of Annie being friendly to me. She was also surprised, as if she wasn't expecting to encounter my social life, even though she knew I had one. She assumes I hook up with girls randomly and thinks Annie might be one of them.

I give her props for recovering so quickly and being gracious with Annie, which is important if she's to represent me. We need to work together without personal entanglements between us or with others who might float in and out of our lives.

The learning experience isn't lost on me. I'd probably react like that if I caught a guy chatting her up. It's bound to happen because men must hit on her at every turn.

My gut and head tell me she's got the hots for me, but she's got her guard up, and I assure myself it's for the best. The season is approaching, and getting someone else to work for me this late in the summer would be a pain. Plus, she lives next door, so it's convenient in more ways than one.

I hate yard work and have a service to handle it. But I find myself pretending to pull weeds when Rachel uses her pool. I can't stop thinking about her and how much I'd love to make a better impression. The sex we had in the storeroom is just a tiny morsel of what I'm capable of, but we can't talk about it because that conversation will lead me down her pants and up her. .. .well, y' know. And she would quit her job, but I look forward to seeing her whenever possible.

While we eat, we take in the ambiance of people around us, laughing and conversing as the warm summer breeze merges them, creating a perfect memory. Our empty plates are taken away, and I grab the bill first.

She raises her eyebrows and sends me an inquisitive look.

"I got this." I plop down a black credit card.

Her head tilts to the side, causing her once straight hair, now wavy from the humidity, to fall around her sweet-heart face.

"You're doing too much."

"I can. Don't worry about it."

She lets out a nervous laugh, and the waitress picks up the check before returning two minutes later for me to sign it.

My signature is unreadable because I don't want anyone to forge it and steal my identity for a credit card. Plus, I sign so many autographs it's caused me to become lax with the letters even though my name isn't as long as some.

"Ready?" I push my chair back to stand.

"Yes, thank you for everything. It was the best food I've had in a long time," she exclaims as she carefully walks across the wooden floors in her heels. Instinctively, I put my hand under her elbow to make sure she doesn't fall.

We return to her place, where I leave my car running, pull her new wardrobe out of the backseat, and hand her the bags with the latest shoes and a purse. I thought jewelry would be a bit much, given she's not my girlfriend or wife. That didn't seem appropriate.

She opens the door, and I follow her inside, checking out her shapely butt in her tight-fitted jeans. She carries her curves well and has no weight to lose. Her skin glows with a late summer tan. It's probably from those daily swims in her brother's pool.

I lay her clothes over the back of a large leather sectional. It's the only piece of furniture in the sparsely decorated living room. You can tell Alexandre was a bachelor until recently.

"I wish I had a pool," I remark, noticing the pool through the wall-to-wall glass doors.

"I am enjoying this place, trust me," she scoffs. "Thank you so much for your help. I can't thank you enough."

"No problem. Pack for the islands. We leave in two days." I turn to go.

"Will do," she replies, beating me to the door before I get close enough to kiss her. I'd love to know how committed she is to these rules. I have her NDA, so if anything were to change organically, I'm covered, and so is she. It would be considered a consensual relationship between two adults: a boss and an employee.

I'm torn and starting to doubt my year-long hiatus from dating. I don't want another relationship simply because it's convenient, and I don't want to settle for just anyone. My crush on Rachel will pass, so we shouldn't complicate things with following our impulses and having more sex. As hot and exciting the sex may have been, what's the use of another indulgence when, clearly, she doesn't want it?

I'll let her hide behind our working relationship for now. If it makes her feel safe and it keeps me from breaking my promise to myself, then so be it.

"Thanks for a nice day. Later." I all but skip out of there as fast as possible. But it's not because I want to leave.

The chemistry we spark when we're near each other gives me a clue that there can be more —much more. If we were together, we would have the opportunity to see where things go. But we're not even considering it because we don't talk about what happened.

These clues of what we could be together are reinforced by storeroom sex and working with her next to me. That first date replays in my head. If I don't watch myself, it will get me into trouble.

If I stayed beside her in her house for one more second, I would have pulled her into my arms, kissed her perfect lips, and carried her to bed to make passionate love to her all afternoon.

So, yeah, I'm relieved when the door closes behind me, shutting out the sweet raspberry lotion on her skin. It's an aroma that makes my nose twitch whenever she enters a room. I've had more blue balls this week than I did as a teenager, and it seems—wrong.

Fuck, she's a hard nut to crack. Right now, she's breaking my balls.

Maybe this magnetic attraction I have for her is in my head, but I'm sure she's fighting the sexual attraction, too. I need to remember just because I want something doesn't mean I get it. I usually have no problem getting what I want from women, but maybe there's a reason we're on the slow burner. I see it when we shoot the shit with each other. I notice her eyes soften as she becomes more relaxed around me, and it gives me hope that she might break her rules.

Rachel can't fake me out with her words when her body knows I'm standing next to hers due to the electricity jumping between us—reminiscent of power cables dangling after an ice storm. It hovers in the air making the hair on my arms rise. Our bodies have a way of throwing sparks when we're together.

Perplexed, I run my hand through my hair. This trip will give us time to think and get to know each other. In the end, it will either make us or break us. I like to bet on sure things, but the outcome is unpredictable this time.

I can't remember the last time I was wrong regarding human behavior. I'm a forward, a right winger, for Christsakes. I read body language for a living—it's how I score and prank the guys so well.

So far, Rachel is mystifying.

I need a suitcase larger than an overnight bag for this trip and find one in my closet. I drag it out and open it on top of my bed. The bed that's sorely lacking a hot chick next door. I should be out with the guys, not pining away for my hot-as-hell assistant, who doesn't act on the attraction we have outside of the workplace either.

Shake it off, Blake.

But all efforts to get Rachel out of my thoughts have so far failed. It's been days since that hot fuck against the wall in the storeroom.

I need her to see something that proves there's more to me than a jock who carries a stick and the player the girls ogle when we walk into a room together.

I'm indecisive while staring at a closet full of dress shirts and custom suits when my mind flips to Rachel in her pretty blue dress. She has a pair of come-fuck-me heels in black, but trust me, I don't need to see her in those to want to fuck her.

The trip to the islands is two days away. I'll need everything from swim trunks for the pool to suits for the formal dinner. But, first things first. I head to the den and grab a stick from the dozen or so I keep in there. I choose one, then rummage through my desk and find markers. Sharpies, to be exact. It's the only permanent marker we use to autograph equipment or photos. I snag it, then toss it in the bag I use to carry hockey sticks.

A text comes in from the other newbie, Simon Korhonen, who is Finnish but speaks English well. He'll be on the first line as a defense this year and just came into the Mauler family from the Ottawa Kings. We met the other day for pictures, and he wants to get together tonight to grab some grub. I agree to dinner as I need to get out and circulate.

Sitting home and percolating over someone I can't have isn't going to help my morale.

It's late afternoon when I hit the gym at the training facility—no sense running all over the place even though there is plenty of open land around here.

I work out, do some weights, and run into another newbie, Wyatt. From what my agent tells me, he's a great forward who is improving daily. I'll get to see for myself when we hit the ice.

It's time to boo-boo, one of my coined phases, so I shower and skate out the door to meet Simon at Mulino's Steak House. It's the finest steak house in town. I wear a blazer over my blue t-shirt to make sure I'm not under-dressed. I do know what places have rules on jackets required for service.

"Simon," I say. I spot him sitting at the bar when I arrive.

He stands, shakes my hand, and I'm reminded he's a big dude. I'm 6'1", but he has a few inches on me. He must have been sizing me up, as well. I picked my clothes well as he's wearing a blazer too.

"Blake." We finish our handshake, and we sit at the bar.

"We're waiting on our table, and I thought we would wait it out here. Take a seat." He leans over the polished redwood bar and asks for a green tea shot. "So, how are you liking Maine?" he asks.

"No complaints so far. But where are all the chicks, man?"

"No clue. There are plenty of waitresses around the arena and girls at Hannigan's who are into fucking hockey players if that's what you want." He chuckles.

"Hmm. I think I know the place you are talking about. The players tend to go there when it's less crowded?"

"You got it. Hard enough keeping the press out of our shit, don't you think?" He gives me a half smile.

"Definitely, they all want their pound of flesh."

"What does that mean, exactly?" He speaks English very well, but it's still his second language.

"Sounds gross, right?" I chuckle. "It means everyone wants a piece of you. They put your face on the cover to sell a magazine, jump out of bushes, and take pictures of you in an embarrassing moment to sensationalize it in the media—we're exploited."

"True, a pound of flesh, that's a good one. I picture gross men beaten up."

I smile, "We feel that way often, don't we?"

"Yes."

Our drinks are set in front of us, and we pick them up to toast. The drink is more than just a straight shot of liquor. It's Jameson Whisky, peach Schnapps, and sour mixed with a spritz of lemon-lime soda.

"Here's to a good season."

"Cheers," I say, and we both down it like we would regular tea on the hottest day of the year.

"God, that's good." I put my empty glass on the bar. It's a smooth drink. The sweet and sour combination covers the alcohol. It also serves as an adequate thirst quencher.

"Yes, it goes down so easily and is perfect for summertime."

We are called for our table. Simon has the tab transferred since we both ordered beers.

"So, ready for training camp?"

"Pretty much. I have a short trip to do a charity event at St. Bart's this week, but I'll be back in time for that first day of hell," I say, smiling because I'm anxious to meet my new teammates. Getting back into the groove of intense conditioning is ball-busting.

"Great, me too, although my two-year-old daughter isn't so happy about it. She loves it here, sees her mother over the Christmas holidays, and takes her to Finland. It's a battle with custody. Her mother is in another country. When the season starts, Daddy is away from home more, so it's tough on her."

"I imagine. I know a bit about not having a mom around. It's tough, man."

"Good kid, I love her to death." I catch a glint in his eye, and it tells me he adores his daughter.

Our waitress comes, and we order. It's nice to get out and not worry about anything other than a great meal, a new friend, and a few drinks to unwind.

Morning comes quicker than I had hoped, considering we had a few more shots. I reach for the aspirin to swallow with a mouthful of water before stretching for my run. As every jock knows, stretching is the key to not getting hurt, and even though we are diligent, injuries still happen.

It's a cool fifty-five degrees when I head out the door, perfect weather to complete a run with a good time. Speaking of a good time, it takes all my willpower to avoid looking for Rachel as I jog past her place. I can't help but feed my desire to see her, especially when I'm not used to hearing 'no' from a woman, and maybe I want what I can't have.

12

RACHEL

The alarm blares and… fuck. Again, it all comes back to me. Of all the men to hook up with, it had to be my boss and my brother's teammate. Last year, I found out Alexandre told all of his friends I was off-limits. This might explain my lonely existence through high school and my need for constant validation.

That pissed me off. How dare he run guys off at a time when every girl dreams of her first love, for fuck's sake. And it sure as hell wasn't Joel! But it might have been a jock on his team back then, and I might have ended up here anyway. Hockey players are interesting since many marry their high school sweethearts.

I throw the light blanket off me and spring out of bed when my alarm goes off. I'd never be up this early if it weren't to check out that God damn beautiful maple tree in the front yard, and by a maple tree, I mean hottie neighbor next door.

With a cup of coffee in hand, I dash to the window, trying not to spill. I need my daily view of Mr. Studly. He's the embodiment of a stud, a man who could tempt a nun to break her vows of celibacy. Thank God I'm not a nun, but boy, do I feel like one.

I catch my breath as he breezes by my window on his way out for a brisk run at dawn.

I don't know how long I can avoid the temptation, but if I get back in the sack with him, I'm going straight to hell because his body is built for sin.

Charlotte's ringtone dings, and I return to my phone on the nightstand.

"Are you okay?" I have to ask because she hates mornings almost as much as me.

"Yes, I was up late last night and read your first few chapters. This is good stuff, Rachel."

For her to call me first thing in the morning is impressive. I wonder if a freight train hit the apartment. Seriously, the woman can sleep through anything.

"When will you be done with it?"

"Don't know. I work on it every night. But Mr. Studly has me going to some charity event in the tropics."

"Hey, you've been wishing for something like this. Maybe all your dreams will come true…in Maine, of all places." She snickers.

"Hey, don't pick on Maine. So far, the locals have no reason to hate me."

"Ah, speaking of haters, have you checked in with your corporate sponsors now that a week has passed?"

"It's probably too soon."

"Never hurts to put a stick up their ass."

"I like Maine, believe it or not. It's quiet and close to Quebec but different enough to appreciate the change of scenery," I say to change the subject.

"Should I sublet your room?"

"I can't afford to pay you if I'm going to get a car. Eventually, my brother will want to have the house for his new family. Whether they live in his house or hers, I don't want to be the third or fourth wheel."

"Right, there is that."

"Yep. Blake surprised me yesterday with an expense account to improve my wardrobe. I don't know if he is being sweet or is embarrassed at how I dress."

"Sweetie, stop assuming everyone thinks the worst of you. My God, you have done nothing to deserve the treatment you've received. Just stop those negative thoughts and reframe them."

"Sounds like you're shrinking me."

"Yes, I am. I've had years of therapy until I started sleeping with the shrink. I've never met another that did so much for me since."

"Slut," I tease.

"Tell me about the clothes shopping after your supposed business lunch yesterday. Do you think Blake likes you?"

"How am I to judge that? You know I haven't a clue when it comes to figuring out anyone's personality, even my own." My voice reflects the solitude I've lived with my entire life.

I'm always on the outside, watching the lives of others while never taking the reins of my life long enough to step out of the box. And when I finally threw caution to the wind, it was with Blake, a man I can't have. I can't compete with his ex even if he wasn't my boss. He can have anyone he wants.

"I read the contract Blake had you sign for his attorney. You're covered with the ND agreement even if you were in a relationship with him."

"Relationship, not a fuckfest."

"It covers that too. Most athletes do these non-disclosure

agreements for anyone alone in a room with them. It's a precaution against being sued in court over nothing."

"Makes sense. I can't say I blame him. I see the way women drool over him. Hell, I drool over him," I scoff.

"Drooling in the middle of sex means he's hit your special spot for tantric sex. I love it."

"What are you doing up this early anyway?"

"Oh, Mr. Wonderful woke me up early with his morning boner," she answers with no shame.

"I knew that. Why did I ask?"

"Because you're kind and thoughtful. If Blake doesn't see that, he doesn't deserve you."

"Right." I stop pacing long enough to jump back in bed and sink into the mattress.

"I'm glad we're in the same time zone."

"Me too."

"I miss you."

"Me too. It's too quiet without you. I don't mind having the extra room if you can't pay the rent. I mean, I'm fine. Mr. Wonderful might be hanging around awhile from the way things are going."

"Seriously?"

"Could be."

"Wow." I'm happy for her, but our two-girl 'band' is breaking up before I have a new BFF or a place to call my own. I'm speechless. I never dreamed we'd be apart so suddenly and our lives would change drastically in less than two weeks. Taking a deep breath, I quietly absorb the finality of our single-girl days. It's sad but inevitable.

"You okay?"

"Yeah. But it sucks. I live next door and see him running outside my window every morning. He was out late last night."

"Oh, look at you, you've graduated to stalking. Congrats," she teases.

"He lives next to me. It can't be considered stalking if I see him coming and going casually. I wouldn't know he came home late, except the headlights of his car hit my bedroom window. Now, whenever he brings home some random puck bunny or model, I witness it in every heart-breaking detail."

"He'll spend half the year on the road," she reminds me.

"Good point. But I need to get on my feet and move out before I crowd my brother. They are newlyweds, after all."

"I get your point. You're going to be fine. You can use this job to get another job. Network on the island with the other pros there, and you can always change where you're living if it becomes unbearable."

"Good point. Moving and rent takes more money than I make. My brother is calling me. Gotta go." I ring off with Charlotte. Talk about a busy morning.

"Hi, Alexandre. How are you?"

"Great, I wanted to know how you were doing."

"Fine, fine."

"Did you meet the new player?"

"Yes, it went fine. He happens to be your new neighbor. You never told me he lives next door to you."

"Wow, I had no idea. He might be renting. I didn't see that coming. Is he nice?"

"Yes, everything is fine. We'll be out of town for a few days…" I hear his voice breaking up from a poor connection before the call disconnects. If it's that important, he'll text me.

I check in with Blake, and it turns out he doesn't need me today, so I use the time to pack. The plan is to leave on Friday and return on Sunday before training camp starts on Tuesday.

I only have one suitcase, so I keep the dresses in their bags to keep them looking fresh. I have no idea what guys do with their suits when they travel, but I'm a fire hazard with an iron in my hand on a good day. There is no way I am messing with an iron at a hotel.

I research packing online and find that keeping my dresses in plastic from the dry cleaners is the way to go, and folding my outfits without overstuffing my bag is the best method.

Great, I grab the car keys and drive to a local luggage store, where I purchase a bag much smaller than the one I have. Besides, I don't want to look like I'm high maintenance. I can rough it like the men.

I pack until I need a break. Lunch is a pre-made salad with canned chicken from the pantry. While in the kitchen, I notice my brother's note on the fridge. Shit, he'll be home when I get back from St. Bart's.

Omg, I better clean the house. I'm not a slob, but I want the house reeking of lavender-scented tile cleaner rather than burned popcorn by the time Callie and Alexandre arrive. By the time I'm done, I'm wiped. Vacuuming this place is a chore. Callie must be neat because my brother was never this tidy growing up.

It's late afternoon by the time I finish packing all the necessities for the trip and lay out my business casual outfit for the flight. I found a printer in the den to print out our itinerary for the charity event. His den doubles as a shrine to his hockey accomplishments. He's pretty fucking impressive.

I'd like to have my claim to fame, but I need to be realistic, which means it may never happen. The book is coming along. I sent more chapters to Charlotte, but I still need more sex scenes, and nothing beats diving into your research for more data. If only…

I could sit around and wish for another night with Blake, but he seems to be sticking to the rules, much to my disappointment.

He's such a flirt, I'm never sure when he's being real. I don't know if I can deal with his long list of exes I might occasionally encounter. That's how it works in their world—vacationing in the most expensive places, attending charity events, and traveling somewhere exotic. For hockey players, they might have one coveted week during the summer for a vacation, then it's back to training and conditioning and sometimes even rehab for injuries.

A player's plate is always full. Maybe I'm not cut out for this life and that's why Blake doesn't pursue me. He said he knows as soon as he meets a woman if there can be something with her. I rely on his expertise, and if nothing is happening between us, it must be for the best.

I eat a frozen dinner and curl up on the couch in the living room. Living here alone for a week staring at the white walls is enough to make anyone panic. This place needs a woman's touch. I hit the remote and watch a romance that happens to be on the channel that offers the weekly dinner and a movie special where they bring on one of the actors from the movie and cook together during the intermissions.

I'm in bed well before midnight and set my alarm. Then I toss and turn and want to see how incredible Mr. Studly will be tomorrow.

❧

Dawn never looked so inviting as I sat next to Blake for the short taxi ride to the airport. The smell of Bay Rum mixed with musk fills my nose. I'm slick between my legs with one whiff of the rum mixed with his scent.

The impulse I have to follow him is overpowering. I've never experienced being mesmerized by anything other than an incredible view of nature or a stunning conclusion to a book that had me gripped to the pages for the climactic ending.

We arrive at the private airport, and after flashing our passports, we're through a door and walk on the tarmac towards a small plane. He leaves our bags at the bottom of the stairs and tells me to climb the steps first. I've never been on a private jet, but I'm immediately impressed with the plush leather chairs and thick, cream-colored carpet.

I'm not sure if a plane for nine people is safe. It's filling up with other players from the team; some of them are quite the sight with their chiseled chins and pretty eyes that swoop over me. They are more human up close than a picture of them taken with a telephoto lens by *Hockey Scoop* magazine or obsessed fans.

I didn't know there would be more than just Blake and I going on this trip, and I'm relieved not to be alone with him, given how much I'd love for him to toss me on the bed and have his way with me—yet I'm disappointed. A part of me wants to throw caution to the wind. I'm young. I can recover from a failed fling.

But my career isn't made of Teflon. A scandal would prolong my hiatus from social media and the money I need to be independent. The book I'm writing is important to me. It's what I've wanted to do since I was a child, but I lacked the courage to put myself out there for another email from a literary agency saying they pass on my manuscript.

My experience with social media makes it possible for me to sell myself and my book. But first, I have to write the book and include erotic scenes.

My obstacle now is the fact that Mr. Dreamy is off-limits, and I need more sexcapades.

Great. I'm stymied as to how to overcome my predicament.

"Hi," I mumble nervously to a cute player as Blake follows me.

OMG, it's Viktor Karlsson, not only the captain of the team but a right-winger. I'd recognize him anywhere with his signature thick brown hair slicked back and draping over his squared shoulders.

He nods as I pass, and I'm so excited I could pee myself.

I keep it under control, smiling and nodding in return.

Finn Callahan, one of the team centers, is also here, sitting with a younger man who screams hockey because he's overdressed for the flight, wearing a form-fitting suit.

"This is my younger brother, James," Finn introduces him as Blake sits beside me, and we buckle our seatbelts.

"Nice to meet you." I lean forward to shake his hand. He's easy on the eyes, and I can tell he and Finn are related. They have the same hair but different eye color. James is not as tall or filled out, given that he must still be in college.

Finn and Viktor are two of the three faces the team promotes endlessly for charity events and fundraisers. . . all-out pretty boys with a squeaky-clean record, as far as I can tell. They're incredibly tight-lipped when it comes to team shenanigans. Loose lips can get players traded or create drama with the wives, and Alexandre says it can tank a team's season.

The pilot tells us to prepare for takeoff, and we're airborne within no time.

I stare at the clouds out the window while Blake talks to the other two players about a vodka commercial. With Blake moving up, maybe he will be in a commercial with them, but it's hard to follow their conversation because James starts asking me questions.

Shit. I want to get to know the seasoned players, not this newbie in a pressed suit, while others discuss important things I want to learn.

Shit, shit, shit.

I'm stuck with the newbie and accept my fate by making the best of it.

"So, where are you from?" he asks.

"Quebec, you?"

"Buffalo. I'm playing college hockey in Boston. They rank as one of the top three colleges for men's hockey."

"Cool. Nothing like a good Northeastern college if you want to go pro."

"Right?" He smiles. Given the good energy vibe we're sharing, I figure we'll be friends, if not contemporaries, for the remainder of the trip. He must be nineteen and volunteered to be Finn's caddy for Saturday's golf event. It's a vacation for James, and they seem to be close by the way Finn is teasing him.

The cabin grows noisy with conversations between players I can't hear. I sit back and enjoy the view as we land on one of the shortest runways in the world and taxi to the tiny airport on St. Bart's.

13

———

BLAKE

I check into the hotel and tell the boys I'll meet them in an hour at the pool. I can't keep my heart from racing, anticipating seeing Rachel up front and personal in her swimsuit later.

We take the interconnected walkway over the water to our bungalow.

"Wow," Rachel gasps as I open the door.

"Nice, huh?"

"No kidding." She rolls her luggage towards a room, and I head to the other, making sure to go around the pool between the rooms and not in it. Falling in would be embarrassing.

"Lunch in an hour at the main pool. Meet me here in forty-five minutes," I say as I walk away.

"Got it!" she hollers over her shoulder.

Ah, this is nice. It's a shame I can't stay here longer, but the off-season is not all playtime. I stayed in LA longer than I should have. I wanted to stick with my trainer and spend some time with my friends because once I left, I knew I'd only see them at weddings or as rivals on the ice. Then, time will pass, and only a few will remain on my phone. That's just the way it is. Life is fast-paced— like the hockey we play.

I hang my suit from the carry-on before rummaging around for my swim trunks and a t-shirt. I change into my pool clothes, step into my Dockers, and meet Rachel at the door a few minutes later.

"This is amazing." Her face lights up as she stands on our front porch overlooking the water. "I've always wanted to visit an island but never imagined it could be this beautiful and the water this blue."

"It matches your eyes," I reply, trying not to stare. She looks like a *Sports Illustrated* model in her two-piece white bikini with a matching sarong tied around her waist. Funny, when I first laid eyes on her, she was as white as Wonderbread, and now seeing her all tan and firm, it takes all my willpower not to take her here and now.

"Let's go," I say, stepping down to the boardwalk that connects the bungalows to the central hotel and amenities.

"Okay." She walks beside me while we both look for signs to steer us toward the pool.

"There it is," she points, "that way."

"Cool, I'm terrible with remembering directions unless I'm driving."

"No way, really? I'm just terrible at directions in general. Sometimes, I overlook the most obvious things in the world. It's quite frustrating."

"I find that hard to believe."

"Oh, it's the truth, all right. That's why I have so many notes on my phone. After a while, I have to spend hours deleting them."

"I thought you were a makeup pro; how do you follow the labels' instructions?"

"It comes naturally to me." She shrugs and adjusts the strap on her tiny black purse, where I assume she keeps her phone and key card.

"So, we have time for a dip in the pool and then. . ." she stops. "What in the world?" Her eyes are fixated on a huge pool with a waterfall.

"It won't bite," I tease.

"Mm, this is so pretty. I'm never gonna want to leave," she says as we walk towards the guys who are waving us over to the loungers they have saved.

"Hey, man." I fist-bump Finn and Viktor. I nod to James.

"Rachel, have a seat, order a drink," Finn suggests.

"Um…" She looks to me for approval.

"I'm ordering, too. Let the beer and shots flow."

"Amen," Viktor replies.

We don't care about what time of day it is. We get our clocks fucked up on the road with all the time changes. Someone once told me they learned in military boot camp that you eat and sleep wherever and whenever you can in order to be ready for the next mission, and in many respects, we do the same.

"Great, then I guess I'll have a margarita," Rachel announces.

Viktor whistles. "Damn, tequila drinks to start. I like this girl already, Blake."

"She's a keeper, for sure." I flick her a grin, and Rachel excuses herself to get pool towels. I can't stop watching her hips sway as she walks in the new wedged sandals I bought for her. I glance at the guys, and they all have their eyes glued on her ass and legs as well.

Fuck me. I bought them to ogle her gorgeous legs, tight ass, and petite feet, not for others to enjoy. Returning my gaze back to Rachel, I lower my sunglasses and stare at her as she grabs a few towels from the stack by the pool. She returns, throws one on my lounger, and then sets hers up as if she's a beach bunny, it's so perfect.

Sheesh. I need a towel to cover up my cock that's got a mind of its own.

"I'm going to get that round of drinks." I excuse myself as I mentally note how many beers I need before heading to the outdoor bar, where I put it all on my tab.

I return, using my fingers to hold numerous plastic cups of brew and the margarita, I observe Rachel. She is engrossed in a conversation about hockey with the guys. I overhear someone asking about her brother.

"Just so happens, he'll be back from his honeymoon when we get home."

"Another one down, man." Finn shakes his head.

When Rachel takes the large frozen margarita from my hand, our fingers brush, sending chills up my spine, and it's not from the cold drink. I hand the plastic cups of beer to the guys, all held by the top with one hand—we're pretty good with our fingers.

"This is heavenly." Rachel sits back with her drink, and I'm confident she's enjoying the sunshine. Every time a guy eyes her like a cat would a mouse. My chest experiences a twang.

I take inventory of her newly painted fingers and toes. It appears she's upping her game a bit. Or maybe I've only seen her on off days.

We may be superficial crass jocks who spend too much time focused on a tiny puck, but we somehow know which girls to take home, which ones to avoid, and which ones are marriage material.

Teammates' sisters are all marriage material, as most of us have a sister or two, and we wouldn't want her to become a name passed around the locker room. It's considered bad form to mess with a player's sister without serious intent to date her exclusively.

Plus, there is a level of protection from her brother should one make a play for his sister because that'll be your last date if you don't treat them right.

I pull a padded wicker lounger beside Rachel's and make light conversation until our drinks are finished. We collectively dip in the pool, resembling a hot tub due to the warm water heated by the tropical sun. I'd welcome some cold water as the hot sun beams on us. We all need to cool off.

Rachel goes under, and when she pops up, I thought the guys would bob their boners. Rachel's hair is now a mess of pale gold and blonde colors, and her pert nipples strain against the white fabric of her wet suit. I need some cold water to shrink my hard-on. I'm positive I'm not the only one with this issue, as plenty of other men are looking, too.

Rachel is the only girl in our group, and I can't have the guys eyeing her gorgeous body, so I create a distraction—I'm protective that way.

"Hey, check out the hottie over there." The guys turn and look at a woman who is spending more money than time on personal trainers, plastic surgery, hair extensions, and dietician-prepared meals.

"Damn, she's in better shape than you, Victor," Finn teases. "Too high-maintenance for me."

"Pass," Viktor volunteers.

"Too old for me," James adds, and his brother splashes water on his face.

"Squirt," he teases.

This starts a water fight until we're all laughing, and we dive under the water as Finn tackles his brother, taking him under with him.

God knows I need some fun.

Afterward, we hang out on the side of the pool, and I catch Rachel slipping her phone back into her tiny purse with a concerned look on her face.

"Everything okay?"

"Oh, yeah, just checking messages."

She's not a good liar.

14

RACHEL

What am I supposed to do? Ashley Hamilton is trending on social media and is here for a swimsuit cover. Does Blake still have feelings for her? Do I tell him? Do I not?

Blake questions me, and I freeze as I did when playing freeze tag as a child. It's funny how life has a way of repeating itself. But I want to break out of my mold of being the girl who gets the leftovers—the girl who's afraid of never being good enough or pretty enough.

With Blake, I experienced something more, and it's bugging the shit out of me that I'm hiding behind the taboo of our working relationship when we both seem transfixed around each other.

To his credit, he hasn't brought any girls home, but I imagine he's tempted. I see the gorgeous girls circling these guys. They remind me of sharks when there's blood in the water because these women want to dine on the juiciest meat.

I don't want a fucking work husband. I want a husband that I desire every minute of every day. Is that even possible? Obtainable? At this point, I'm so horny I can sense Blake is near me even before he says a word. I long for his touch. Hell, I'd settle for him to accidentally bump into me.

I should tell him Ashley is on the island, but what if he still cares for her? I know little about their relationship. He told me his version of the breakup, but Ashley's version will undoubtedly differ. There will always be his side, her side, and the truth somewhere in the middle.

Does she still love Blake?

What if she wants him back?

Unsure of what to do, I play it cool; that's what jocks do. We're having a good time—no need to spoil it.

But I know she's here, and it sucks to be me right now.

I'm the paper in a game of rock, paper, scissors. If I don't tell him, it will make me look like the jealous type. I'm not one to keep secrets, other than the book I'm writing, because that's my personal life.

However, hiding this information from Blake isn't me. I'm being sketchy, and my conscience is getting the best of me.

He's a grown man; he can take care of himself. I wouldn't be thrilled if Joel surprised me with an unscheduled visit. And if Blake knew about it, I would want him to give me a heads-up.

Between the warm pool and frozen margaritas, I'm having a great time with all the guys. Am I the only girl on this circuit from the Maulers?

"Oh, look over there." James points. It's another athlete, a football player, and James is creaming in his pants over him.

This weekend, It looks like a who's who of world-class jocks. I wonder if Ashley is part of the charity event or if it is just a coincidence that she's here.

"Good turnout for the golf tournament," I comment, having no idea who the player is, even after James says his name and rattles off his stats. His brain generates information like the old hard drives. "I never paid much attention to the Make a Kid Smile organization before," I continue, "but I hear they do incredible things for sick kids."

"Yes, it is. We're here to raise money and grant wishes," James adds as if he knows more about the trip than me.

I never imagined jocks would be excited to see other jocks. However, the look on James' face says it all. He's young, and apparently, this trip is his first opportunity to see this many star athletes in the same place at the same time, so it's a big deal for him.

I can't think of anyone I would want to meet, but that doesn't stop me from wearing my dark sunglasses to check out all the hot bodies poolside. Even with all the man meat around, my eyes circle back to Blake. I catch him looking my way but brush it off as he's probably wondering why I'm still hanging around.

I'm drying off by my lounger when Blake swings by, and I ask him to adjust the umbrella for me. I can't have sun damage on this face; it would be bad for my business touting the latest skincare and makeup products.

I hold the hotel-provided, one-time-use tube of sunscreen in my hand.

"You need help with that?"

"That would be great." And as soon as the words leave my mouth, I realize all too late it might not be the best idea given our chemistry.

I hand the tube to him, and there is no way to prepare for his strong hands, meticulous with the sunscreen, as my vagina is quivering in anticipation. Thank God it's a small tube because I'm grinding my teeth, and my hands grab the towel while I clamp my mouth shut. I'm ready to orgasm in public.

When I'm about to let loose, he stops.

Thank you, Mother of God.

"Thanks." My voice is breathless and weak.

"No problem," he says, wrapping a towel around himself. I can't help but notice the tent he's covering up.

He moves back to his friends while I lean back and take in the sights of the older men dressed head to toe in Tommy Bahama shorts, and he's standing around the large bar, a drink in one hand and a cigar in the other. They're conversing with the over-tanned young woman who looks like she's been on this circuit before.

Flirting is the second sport this weekend, and there will undoubtedly be sports between the sheets later for some lucky gals. For all I know, Ashley might be walking around here as well.

The player, James, drops by to chat with the guys. Their tall silhouettes stretch into elongated shadows as it gets late. Someone mentions they're getting hungry, and we all agree to leave the pool and get ready for dinner.

We say goodbye to the gang and head toward our bungalow. I'm weighing whether to tell Blake that Ashley is on the island. I'm sure Blake is on to me lying earlier when he prods me with questions.

"So, what's up? You seemed concerned earlier. Did you hear from Joel or your brother? Everything okay at home?"

"Um. No, well. Maybe? I don't know if you want to know, but Ashley is on the island, too."

There, it's out in the open at last.

Whew.

"Really? Well, thanks for the heads up."

"Yup." I can't even look at him. If he's pining away for someone else, and I see it, my weekend vacation is ruined. And with it—the ending to my book.

"I tell you what, if we see her, let's act like we're a hot

couple. This will prevent me from slipping back into old bad habits."

"Sure." My reply flies out of my mouth before I contemplate what he asks of me. I blow it off as a non-event. What are the odds of running into her? Besides, I didn't see social media advertising the Maulers being here. I assume she won't know he's here unless I missed something.

"But you'll owe me," I put it out there. Who knows where he has connections? It doesn't hurt to keep my options open if this PA job fails.

I'm new to this and how his media works. Maybe the team has back channels that I'm not privy to. For all I know, Blake might have found out about Ashley being here on his own. In the meantime, I've made points.

"Great, we'll head to the main hotel for dinner, run over tomorrow's agenda, and maybe we can have some fun when I'm off the clock. No sense passing up an opportunity to enjoy the island. Right?"

We arrive at our bungalow, and Blake uses his keycard. The fact I think it's 'ours' is unnerving. I've never cared for any man enough to want to spend this much time with him.

"Thanks," I say as I sail past him and make a point to inhale deeply, and I do so I can catch a whiff of his cologne. I'm overflowing with sexual tension. The butterflies in my stomach are doing overtime; making food is the next move, a welcomed idea.

"I'll change for dinner," I call over my shoulder as I walk around our private pool.

"Gotcha. Is thirty minutes enough time?"
"Plenty," I fib.

I t's close to sunset, and the path is now lit with tiki torches as we follow the wooden signs to the resort's restaurant.

I pause to stare at the setting sun, and a warm, ephemeral breeze passes over us, giving me goosebumps. Captivated by the view, we're impervious to others walking by.

"It's breathtaking. I've never been this far south." As the waves lap the shore, the sun dips to the horizon, a ball of golden hues. The sea is now indigo, with hints of cerulean tipping the foam-topped waves.

"Yeah, it's the magic of the islands," he says, looking deep into my eyes before taking my hand. "Come, let's eat. I'm hungry."

"Gee, we forgot lunch, didn't we?"

"Yeah, I think I drank mine." He chuckles.

Before jumping in the shower, I snacked on some nuts from the mini bar and down a water bottle. It's nice not having to worry about the price of snacks.

I've never stayed in a place this nice with lavish perks. The dining room at the restaurant reminds me of something you'd see on a cruise ship with the white pressed tablecloths, lit candles, and wicker back chairs that match the island's tropical vibe.

Blake gives his name to the maître d', and we mill around on the outside patio waiting for our table. We're checking out the local artwork on the walls when our conversation is interrupted by a woman's voice, too loud to be missed, calls, 'Blake' as she pushes her way through the crowd.

15

BLAKE

So far, the trip has been incredible. I've been able to spend one-on-one time with Rachel and get to know the person behind the brilliant blue eyes and plump, kissable lips.

When she walked into the pool wearing that white bikini, my cock jumped to life. She's as sexy as a swimsuit model without all the fuss. Sure, I swore off dating women for at least a year, but that promise is getting harder to stick to—it's more like a sticky note that's been ruined and keeps falling off my wall calendar. The likelihood of keeping our relationship strictly professional isn't boding well for me.

I want to nip at her lips, lick her pussy and feel her under me as I thrust into her repeatedly. I want to hear her call out my name when she comes. As her boss, I understand her predicament, and I'm trying to respect her wishes. She needs this job and doesn't want to disappoint her family. I get it.

When she tells me that my ex, Ashley, is on the island, I know it's only a matter of time before we bump into her. This place isn't big enough to evade anyone for any length of time.

As tourists and jet-setters, we all tend to hit the same places at the same time of year.

Rarely do we go anywhere alone. We all meet at these social functions to reconnect with old friends and make new ones. It's also a way to fill the void of being away from our loved ones on these trips. It's a fleeting and fake plug for the hole in my heart left by a mother. Ashley didn't help matters. No matter how many women I date, it all falls apart, like clockwork, after a year.

It's always been difficult for me to trust women, but Rachel is different. She's honest, even going so far as to admit her life is a colossal fuckup. But I don't think she's a loser because some old boyfriend sabotaged her career. She is doing her best to survive one of the unpleasant realities that life dishes out.

My take on Rachel is that she needs support to boost her confidence. She needs to be around people who believe she's worthy of having nice friends, clothes, and vacations. If they believe in her, she will, too.

For now, she's doing what it takes to reach her goals and remain independent, and I have to give her the space to grow. Meanwhile, I yearn to give her more, so much more. I'm not sure how to impress her without scaring her off.

Personally, becoming successful not only takes dedication to learn your skill, but it also requires luck. If I was injured the year I was picked up, or right after, I might not be where I am now. I trained hard, found an agent who believed in me, and beat the odds.

Training season and life on the road is brutal. I often dodge fans and the press during the season when I'm out and about.

Hockey isn't over just because it's summer. Off-season is a funny term because it's not free time. It's time to rest, rehab if injured, work on improving special skill sets, and continually work to be better, stronger, and faster. We manage to throw in weddings and vacations, having fun with our families and friends.

In the long run, it's easier for me to put time in at the gym every week rather than let myself go. I have no desire to experience the discomfort of retraining my muscles that have been on vacation too long. We don't get much of a break from our jobs as it's a part of who we are.

I'm waiting with Rachel outside the restaurant when the hair on my back stands up like a black cat scared by a witch on a broomstick.

Someone is calling my name. I'd know that voice anywhere. It's Ashley.

Fuck. I hoped it wouldn't happen this quickly. I wanted more time with Rachel before my ex surfaced like a huge pimple.

I slowly turn. "Ashley." I give her a polite hug as she pulls me to her and gives me a peck on the lips that makes me uncomfortable.

"I can't believe we're both here. My goodness, it's been months since I've heard from you."

Take a hint, I've deleted your number, I want to say, but I hold my tongue and give her a polite smile.

"This is my girlfriend, Rachel. Rachel, this is Ashley."

"Nice to meet you," Rachel says, going first.

"Hm. You too." Ashley barely looks at Rachel, dismissing her and returning her laser-like focus to me.

Shit.

But I gladly take the heat to prevent her from getting her hooks in Rachel.

"I didn't believe it when I read your name on the list of attendees for the charity event, so of course, I had to say yes when I was offered a modeling job here. Who can beat the white sand? It's like when we went to The Biltmore in Santa Barbara." She raises her designer sunglasses and gives me her award-winning smile that could launch a million ships, only it's not working on me like it used to.

My name is called again, only now it's by the host. I wrap my arm around Rachel's waist to escort her. I'm also being a bit possessive, but we're a couple in front of Ashley.

"Oh, can you make that three? We're all friends, right Blakey?"

And just like that, Ashley crashes into my life again. Thank God I have a backup plan. I knew she broke up with her boyfriend a month ago, and I had a feeling she'd find a way to cross paths with me.

I look to Rachel for guidance, and she cocks her head in Ashley's direction and says, "That would be great."

I gulp and try not to choke on my saliva. Will Ashley buy our fake relationship?

"This way, please," the maître d' says, leading us to a table for four.

I pull the chair out for Rachel, who slides her hands down the back of her white mini-dress and has a seat.

"How is your shoot going?" Rachel asks, placing a linen napkin in her lap.

"Oh, great, the beaches are so relaxing compared to the pressure from the staff and a photographer who can be obnoxious, taking way too many pictures. I'm exhausted by the time they call it quits for the day. I have an evening shoot coming up, so I can't eat much, but I'd love to have a Skinny Girl martini."

Rachel holds back a smirk. It's such a typical model move. I find it funny, too. I suppress my chuckle. My eyes meet Rachel's over the menus placed before us. Our waiter takes over the conversation, and I couldn't be more relieved.

Ashley is on her best behavior, but I'm already drained of energy.

Rachel requests a regular iced tea, but I need something stronger to get through this and order a gin and tonic.

"So, what have you two been up to? How long have you been together? Curious minds want to know and all that." She runs a hand through her hair to show off her gold bangle bracelets.

Ashley's questions sound sweet, but her look is anything but. When I meet her gaze, it's as if she's throwing razor blades at me instead of daggers. She's pissed and going for the jugular.

Our drinks arrive.

Part of me knew she'd want me back, so Rachel is my backup plan for any ex or potential woman who may have ulterior motives. I saw the way they worked the pool earlier, and I'm not surprised. As my career has advanced, I can't deny the uptick in the caliber of women interested in me.

I'm not a stranger to the culture. Moving up to the pros, I've become accustomed to people making promises and not keeping them. Plenty want more from me than I want to give, whether it's in business or pleasure.

"We recently met. Y'know how it is, a hot as fuck hookup in a semi-public place. It's quite the rush and very addicting," Rachel responds as she circles her finger suggestively around the rim of her iced tea.

I didn't expect that answer, but it looks like Rachel is not about to take smack from my ex. This puts a grin on my face. I can't help but admire her balls-to-the-wall answer— literally.

The cost of admission to see Ashley's jaw drop is… well, priceless. She swallows half of her martini in one gulp.

"There's just something about Rach. Y'know what they say, when you meet the right one, you know in your gut that you've met your soulmate."

"Soulmate," Ashley scoffs, draining the rest of her drink. She twirls the stem of the martini glass between her perfectly manicured fingertips. "What do you do, Rachel?"

"I used to be in PR, and currently, I'm helping Blake."

"Your accent, Canadian?"

"Yes."

"Hm. That must make dating difficult if you can only be in the States for half the year. The season is tough on relationships. I should know."

"We'll work it out," I interject.

"It just seems like you've become serious so—quickly. The Blake I know takes his time before getting into a serious relationship." Her eyes fix on Rachel, waiting for her to crack.

I slide my hand under the table and gently rub Rachel's thigh until I see her back arch. Then, I lean over and deliver a passionate kiss but pull away when she pushes her soft lips into mine with meaning. I couldn't be happier.

Her response hardens my cock and reminds me of our hot hookup. It wasn't a one-time thing because those thoughts, feelings, and hormones are still alive. Everything from that night, the work meeting, and fingertip brushes in public come rushing back, making it even more difficult to pull away.

Rachel's lips are warm, and I want to nibble on them, not my ex, which I'm convinced poses no threat to my bachelor status.

Rachel, on the other hand, is another matter.

"We've found communication to be important, among

other things." I shrug, meeting Ashley's eyes, giving her back the line she gave me when I left her. She mentioned how I wasn't including her in my life. She blamed me for ruining hers and holding her back. From the look on her face, she's not liking what I'm delivering.

I've moved on and don't know who's more shocked. Her pretty face and perfect body do nothing for me. What we had is dead and buried.

As for Rachel, I want her in my corner and my bed. Baby steps are working to keep her close, yet we remain at arm's length. It's impossible to ignore my bad-boy thoughts of taking her to as many locations of our bungalow as possible. But I want to drill her like an enforcer on the team, hard enough to feel it on my body for days. I want her sweaty body clinging to mine as we move together and hear her beg for more when I'm pounding into her.

Now, if I can only get through this dinner, I promise myself it will be worth the blue balls putting a damper on the Porterhouse steak on my plate.

16

RACHEL

Of course, I'm intimidated by a top model with not one ounce of body fat. Who wouldn't be? She's as tall as Blake, and I can't help but think they must've made a stunning couple. I, on the other hand, look like a child standing next to him.

When she surprised us outside the restaurant, I assumed she'd have Blake eating out of her hand before dessert, but to my surprise, that did not happen. Hmm. What went down between them?

I'd love to ask her, but I didn't think she'd send me a friend request on social media soon. If anything, she looked at me as if I was an insect she needed to exterminate. So yeah, I imagine she can be a real bitch when crossed.

Women like her are not born; they are made. You can blame the cruel, cutthroat world she's had to survive in order to get where she is in her career. Or, she might be that person in real life.

We've all seen enough episodes of *Dance Moms* or *Toddlers and Tiaras* to know the twisted world these girls grow up in. The thick skin they develop is built-up scar tissue from all the catfights and backstabbing.

Ultimately, we all carry scars, mine from my absentee parents and more recently, my asshole of an ex, Joel.

I'm not sure if Ashley will buy this fake romance with Blake. However, I'm willing to help him sell it. Hell, I might even have some fun while I'm at it.

At dinner, I sip my tea and watch Blake work his magic. Sitting tall, he exudes confidence and no longer looks panicked like when Ashley called his name earlier. When he leaned towards me for the kiss, it erased all doubts that I could keep this relationship working. I wanted to slip off my panties then and there. What am I to do? He wants a fake relationship. I want a real one.

Ashley said her goodbyes shortly after she lost her appetite, watching Blake spoon-feed me tiramisu for dessert.

I guess she got the message.

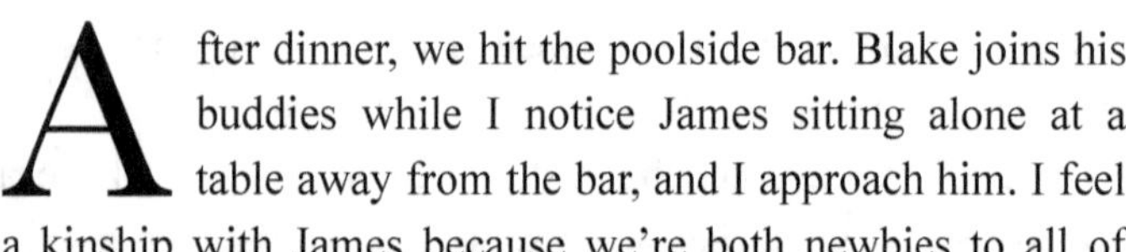

After dinner, we hit the poolside bar. Blake joins his buddies while I notice James sitting alone at a table away from the bar, and I approach him. I feel a kinship with James because we're both newbies to all of this.

"So, you're Finn's caddy tomorrow morning?" I ask, pulling up a chair next to him.

Looking up from his beer, he replies, "Oh, yeah. He takes his golf game very seriously. You want a drink?"

"Sure, I'll have a tequila sunrise. Seems fitting, right?"

"It does." He smiles and gets the bartender's attention.

"What are you doing tomorrow? By the way, are you and Blake together? I wasn't sure," he asks.

"Hm. I can't discuss it, the NDA—y'know."

Thank God I'm getting faster at dodging questions, especially when I'm not even sure how to answer them. If I told him the truth and Ashley found out, I'd be betraying Blake.

"That sucks, but I hope we can be friends, no matter what." He walks a few steps to the bar, grabs my drink, and hands it to me. I bet this just went on his brother's tab.

I need to be careful not to lead James on with anything flirtatious. I will admit, Elle from *Legally Blonde*, who knew every trick in the dating handbook, taught me everything I know about flirting.

The outdoor lighting is not the best, but I can see he has similar hazel eyes, only greener, the same dark hair, and thick eyebrows like Finn.

"I can tell you and Finn are related. I don't know your brother, but you have the same facial features. I don't know any of the team players, except my brother, Alexandre."

"Oh, no way!" he exclaims.

I know he's running Alexandre's stats through his head, and he starts listing them, then realizes he's talking too much and apologizes.

I smile. "It's fine. I need to get used to that now that I'm living in Maine."

I take a few sips from the drink in my hand, and when I look up, I notice Blake coming around the corner of the bar looking peeved.

Shit.

My swallow is more air than a cocktail. I cough and sputter.

"Are you okay?" James asks as I lightly pound my chest, trying not to draw attention to my cleavage.

"Yes." Oh shit. Blake is observing me, and he doesn't look happy.

"Oh, there you are, Rachel. I've been looking for you." Is it my imagination, or does Blake's face soften when he realizes I'm only having a drink with James?

"Hey, what's up?" I ask.

"I'd like to go, and I want to walk you back to our room. You can't be too careful, even here."

"Oh." I sputter, surprised he's pretending like we're a couple in front of James. Shit, now the team will think I'm nothing more than a puck bunny.

James nods and lifts his beer to let us know he understands.

I toss my plastic cup into the nearest trash can and bid James goodnight. "Good luck tomorrow." I wave.

I turn to Blake.

"What's up with that? I don't know when we're pretending to be dating and when we're not, so I didn't say anything to James."

"Thank you, sorry. I don't mean to be a jerk, but I have to get up early tomorrow, and it will be a long day. Since I have some free time in the afternoon, I thought you might want to book something fun for us to do. I'd love to break away for some alone time."

"Sure. I'll look into it in the morning." I can barely keep up; he's walking so fast.

"What's up? Did Ashley text you?" We reach our bungalow in record time, and I wait for him to flip on the light because all we have is the glow from the lights in the pool.

"No, actually," he says, then he turns to me. "Thanks for playing along and having my back at dinner. You were great. And thanks for not telling James about our, um, arrangement."

"Well, I'm calling in a favor eventually," I remind him.

Maybe he has a contact that can be a stepping stone to a real career for me if my book idea goes tits up. If not, I've seen and done things with him that I'd never get to experience otherwise.

Let's not forget he's given me plenty of material I need for my story. I'm storing all the details in my memory bank and notes for what I hope will be a series of books.

"Sure, whatever I can do," he says, flipping on the lights and dimming them in our room. "I apologize for being abrupt when I spoke to you when you were talking with James."

"It's fine. I'm kind of off the dating market for the weekend," I reply, sounding a bit disappointed.

Thinking about it, if I wasn't busy pretending to be his girlfriend, I could be hooking up and doing all kinds of "research" for my book. There are plenty of hot men here and plenty of opportunities.

I turn to my room, but his hand catches mine, and he pulls me towards him. I'm inches from his chest and close enough to feel his body heat.

"Yeah, well, about that," he says, and his firm lips descend on mine. I feel dizzy and lightheaded, like when I stand up too quickly. I can't tell if it's from the tequila or him mixed with the salty night air that has me suspended in time.

My mouth melds with his, kisses as hot as fired steel become one. His tongue is in my mouth, searching, pressing, upping the pressure in me as his need becomes more urgent. I feel his hard cock pressing against my stomach, and I know what he wants.

Stepping backward to catch my breath, I lose my balance, but his arms wrap around me, pulling me back to him. I wonder what happened to light his fire. Then it occurred to me he was jealous of James tonight.

"What. . ."

"Shhh." He puts his finger against my lips, unzips the back of my dress, and slips the straps off my shoulders, letting it fall in a heap at my feet.

"You're beautiful. Do you know that?"

I'm stunned.

He runs his hands through my long hair, and I unbuckle his belt and let it drop.

Tit for tat.

I pull his zipper down, and he kicks his pants away as he pulls off his polo.

We slip out of our shoes, and I'm still in my lacy undies and bra. The bra is off with a flick of a hand before he kneels in front of me and tugs my undies down with his teeth.

Holy mother of God.

17

BLAKE

I knew it was over with Ashley. I just had to be sure. Hence the big lie Rachel helped me pull off. Tonight's trip down memory lane proved that Ashley was never "the one."

If I learned anything tonight, it's that I cannot kiss Rachel without wanting to fuck her. When I kissed her, and she kissed me back, it rocked me hard, and suddenly, I didn't want to fake a damn thing.

I couldn't let her walk to our room alone and miss an opportunity for my cock to be in her pussy. When I found her drinking and chatting with James, I let my jealousy turn me into an asshole. Funny, I've never been territorial over a woman before.

Rachel seems oblivious to all the guys circling and checking her out, but I notice it. James is a friendly kid and not a threat. I don't know why I overreacted. I didn't plan on telling anyone but Ashley that we're a couple, but I, for some reason, needed to mark my territory when I saw her with James. Now James will tell Finn, and the gossip will spread faster than an STD at training camp.

When we get to our bungalow, I can no longer ignore the electricity that runs like a river between us and figure it's go big or go home. Taking her hand, I pull her towards me, and our lips meld together. I slip my tongue into her warm mouth. Her fingers trail gently up my neck, and shivers go up and down my spine.

I take my shirt off and nibble on her neck. She reciprocates with her tongue at the apex of my shoulder and runs it down to my nipple, taking it between her sweet lips and suckling me as if I'm a juicy piece of prime rib.

Kneeling before her, I take her panties off with my teeth and toss them. I run my hand down her shapely leg, close my eyes, and enjoy her smooth skin and essence as I take my time getting to her foot. Lifting her foot, I gently knead the bottom of them with my strong fingers and listen to her gasp and moan.

I like pleasing her, so I do the same to her other foot. Done, I put her foot down and lick her from her knee to her pussy and take in all its sweet nectar. She supersedes the tiramisu dessert we just ate.

She guides my head with both hands and pulls at my dark blond hair as she withers with pleasure. I lift my head enough to witness her enjoying the foreplay. Her back is arched, and her grip on my hair is an anchor.

I run my tongue up her taut abs, her muscles flexing involuntarily. Her body quivers as she lets out a soft giggle. She's ticklish. I sit back on my heels, knowing she's melting like butter under my caresses.

"We shouldn't," her words are barely audible.

"By morning, everyone will assume we're together; why waste another minute?" is all the encouragement I need to give her.

"Hmm," she moans against my chest, kissing and sucking

my nipple as her other hand pulls on the hair over my sternum. Our lips meet again, and I take a deep breath of her. She's berries, mingled with dampness on her skin, and the combination feeds my insatiable need for her.

She feeds the adrenaline in me, and it's like making a game-winning shot on goal. This is what it's like having her touch me back, fanning the flames between us. The undeniable chemistry from the first time we met always warms me, but tonight, she's setting me on fire.

Suddenly, I have the immature needs of a teenager, with the undeniable urge to take her as soon as possible. I want to reach out and tweak a nipple just because it's there, whether we are at the arena or in public. I want her constantly.

She pulls back. "No, we can't do this, as much as I want to. . ."

Her sense of responsibility surfaces again, and she gently pushes me away, but it's not enough to deter me.

I silence her with my lips, claim hers, and she kisses me back. Our hands feverishly run over each other's bodies like we can't get enough of each other. Her hand grabs my hard cock, making my heart race like a Formula 1 car. Good thing I went commando tonight.

She runs her hand up my shaft, then down, caressing the head. My eyes close, and my back arches backward. I'm harder than a wooden hockey stick. I could explode at any minute, but I won't do that. I hold back, I want to make tonight last, and the consequences be damned. I can't stop.

I've waited for this moment ever since our first hookup. I want it to be special this time, so I sweep her up in my arms and carry her to my bed, laying her down in the spot I jerked off last night to visions of her naked body.

Now, I have her in the flesh, on her back, the full moon casting its glow over her bare skin. Our eyes meet briefly before I drop kisses, like raindrops, here and there, then more concentrated like a heavy rainstorm. I cover her bountiful breasts with kisses and nip at her nipples, causing her to squirm and breathe heavily in a fit of desire and anticipation.

Running her soft hands over my shoulders, a finger trails over the scar on my right shoulder where I tore it to shreds in high school, skating into the boards to make a goal. Her touch effectively helps to erase the memory of my excruciating pain.

I lean over to the nightstand and grab some Fuck Sauce, strawberry flavored, and drip it on her breasts, gently rubbing it over her nipples as they harden under my touch.

Her breath is the only sound in the room as she inhales air, arches her back, and closes her eyes while I take my time licking the strawberry flavor off her breasts.

Goosebumps run up my spine as if a draft blew into the room. Damn, her body is built perfectly for me, and my mission is to give her the works, to make sure she'll never forget tonight. I don't want her to ever look at another man the way I want her to look at me.

I take my cock in hand and rub it against her pussy lips and clit, then pull away, teasing her, leaving her writhing on the sheets. She grasps my shoulders, her nails like claws, pulling me towards her as she whimpers. She lifts her hips into the air to get more of me.

When I deny her, she pinches my nipples and tugs the hair around them, and I must admit I like the unnecessary roughness.

I slip inside her just enough to show her how hard I am, then pull out.

She slaps me across the cheek.

"What's that for?"

"You tease!"

"You have no idea." With a wicked grin, I slide my hand under her sweet ass and lift her high enough to take her in one plunge, causing her to gasp and moan.

"Oh my God," she claws at the bedsheets and lifts her hips higher to meet me, and I thrust into her again. Her hands slap the bed as she twists and moans uncontrollably under me.

"Say it," I implore her.

"What?"

"What do you want?"

She says nothing. I pull back, leaving only my tip inside her. She pushes her hips forward, chasing my cock, but I back up just enough to frustrate her.

"Say it," I tease.

Rotating around her engorged labia, I can tell she wants my cock so bad it's driving her crazy.

"You, damnit," she says, conceding before dropping her hips to a comfortable position. I plunge in, moving faster and faster as the tension builds and her Kegel muscles clinch around my hard as fuck cock, and just as she peaks, she grabs a fistful of my hair and pulls hard enough to make it hurt. The brief pain adds to my pleasure and pushes me over the edge as we explode together.

Her bellows of 'ah' and 'mmm' are so loud it could register on a Richter scale as another wave overtakes her one last time.

As I come, I throw my head back and let out my own 'ah.' I'm still hard, and we both experience another tiny quake of pleasure before we're spent.

I crumple beside her, my muscles tired by the one endeavor with no rival. No one can make me insane with desire like Rachel.

We catch our breath, and I pull her to me, although we're

damp and sticky with sweat, lube, and the increasingly humid night air.

"I'm hot. Let's use the pool," I say, helping her out of bed and leading her to the one in our bungalow.

"Jump," I yell, holding her hand and jumping.

She leaps in with me and pops up beside me, her wet hair barely covering her breasts.

She trusted me. My lips claim hers, and round two is building.

Rachel understands business. She has her own company, and so do I. Now we're in business together. By that, I mean she helps me dodge my ex, and I'll make it up to her later. In the meantime, I'm happy to have her all to myself.

We're taking baby steps but progressing in the right direction. However, I'd be an idiot to believe that anything after tonight will be easy.

18

RACHEL

The sex—mind-blowing. The buildup, the much-needed release to satisfy the overpowering attraction between us, the Fuck Sauce, and the refreshing pool afterward, all divine. I'm in heaven and plan to enjoy this as long as it lasts, knowing this is unsustainable and at some point, there will be a price to pay.

Life doesn't work out for me like it does for others. Sure, I'll be crushed when the romance ends, but I'm a big girl, and this will all be worth it. I wish I could thank his Scandinavian ancestors for his Viking warrior body, dark blond hair, and light blue eyes. Sadly, no man in my future will be able to top this.

We're still in our pool when he pulls me into his arms and says, "Take a breath."

I barely have a chance to get a lungful of air before he pulls me under the blue-lit water. I open my eyes; we kiss, exchanging air between our lips before we surface. He swims to a ledge in the shallow end, taps a button, and the spa jets kick in. I sit beside him and let the jets massage my back.

This will help to avoid any kinks in my back after getting

drilled by someone so muscular and large—like everywhere large. Blake puts considerable force behind his thrusts. I've never been, well, banged so hard before, but I loved it. What's the use of having that body if he won't use it off the ice, too?

I can't wait to text Charlotte later; she'll be all ears.

"How about something to drink?"

"Sure," I reply dreamily, staring up at the stars covering the sky like a blanket of sequins through the skylight that retracts.

He steps out and returns with a bottle of champagne and two plastic flutes. I watch him pop the top and pour the bubbly. Leaving the bottle on the deck, he hands me a drink and slides back into the pool.

"I can see how one can get used to this," I muse, sipping the champagne.

"Work hard, play harder, is what I say. Now, what shall we toast to?"

"I don't know," I answer, not knowing what 'this' is.

"To new friends," he says, tapping my flute with his.

"To new friends." I smile, but inwardly, I cringe. I'm in the friend zone. Fucking friends?

"So, tell me about this side hustle or long-shot plan you mentioned when I met you?"

The buzz of the bubbly hits, and I spout off like a whale.

"Oh, I'm writing a romantic comedy. I have a degree in creative writing, and it's been a dream of mine to write and publish as many books as possible and make a living at it. A long shot, I know."

I shrug my shoulders as if to say it's a crazy idea.

"So, you are creative. I think that's cool. How long before the book is completed?"

"I'm about three-quarters of the way through. I've sent

the finished chapters to my old roommate, Charlotte. She's a copywriter and has some connections. If I'm lucky, I might get an agent. It's in the infant stages and still a pipe dream."

"No, it's not. These things take time and some luck, but you'll get there."

"Really?" With the fuzzy buzz of alcohol in my brain, I look at him and want to stay with him here, like this, for all eternity.

"Yeah, I mean, look at me. I did the same thing to get into the NHL, years of work and sacrifice."

"Trust me. I'd rather try and fail than do nothing and regret it later."

"Right. So go for it."

"I am. Who knows, maybe one day you can say, you knew me when. . ."

"Exactly. Being a PA is fine for now, but you're capable of much more, Rachel."

"Thanks."

"I'm getting soggy. Let's move back to the bedroom, take a hot shower, and finish this bottle."

He helps me out of the pool, and I follow him, checking out his gorgeous, rounded ass cheeks. I'm mesmerized by his thick thighs and watch the muscles on his back move as he walks.

He can tell I'm a little tipsy, and he helps me into the open shower, where we stand under the warm water coming down like rainfall. He gets a squirt of shower gel and glides it over my body, paying particular attention to my tender girlie parts.

I do the same, lathering up his broad chest and back. Without looking away from his gaze, I caress his balls and buttocks before moving down his thick legs, feeling the solid muscle mass under my fingertips. Reaching his feet, I lift them and gently massage each one, knowing it was erotic when he did that to me. He closes his eyes and moans, enjoying it as much as I did.

We rinse off, and he wraps a fluffy white towel around his waist and grabs another towel to dry me. I've never had anyone pay this much attention to me, and it's what I imagine a honeymoon would be like.

I take the towel from him and dry his back. We grab our drinks and return to his room, darker now that the moon is high and no longer shining through the window. He helps me into the elevated bed, crawling behind me like he's the hunter and I'm the prey.

Pulling me into his lap, he refills our flutes.

"I'm impressed. I had no idea you were such a romantic."

"Why not? This is my last getaway before a grueling season. I'm on a new team, and there's a lot of pressure to produce goals because the new owner, Greg Anderson, wants the cup."

"Of course, every team does. The Maulers have more depth now, so we'll have to see how that works out. Plus, you can always use some luck," I add.

Winking, he says, "I think I have all the luck I need."

We talk, kiss, and laugh the night away until we've killed two bottles.

I drift off in his arms just before sunrise. He wakes me a few hours later with kisses that make me want him again. I had no idea I could be so horny for more cock.

Needless to say, we enjoy another spicy round.

I hope I'll be able to walk after this.

When they say take one for the team, it's never just one.

I'm like a princess waiting for the sun to come up and the magic spell to wear off, returning me to my other life as his assistant.

We take a quick shower together before he heads to his morning golf event. As soon as he leaves, I book us a horseback ride on the beach for later in the day. With nothing else to do, I take my laptop to the pool and catch a few more rays.

And like a turd in the toilet, Ashley drops by. Of course, what could be worse than going toe to toe with Blake's ex when he's not here to referee?

"Well, don't you have the flow of a rock star?"

I pretend to be busy on my laptop, which I am, and take my time acknowledging her.

"Hi, Ashley. So nice to see you." I lie, and why not? Everything lately seems to be one lie after another.

"I just wanted to drop by to say don't come crying to me when he ditches you. He's got commitment issues, so don't get your hopes up that you'll be the one to fix him."

"Never crossed my mind."

"Forewarned is forearmed," she coos, spinning like she's at the end of some runway. "Later." She waves goodbye as she struts away.

What the hell is that supposed to mean? What have I gotten myself into? And what does she know that I don't?

19

BLAKE

The golf tournament wasn't so bad. It even had its moments of fun. Sadly, it will be my last time on the green for the season, unless we get a few days' break in the action. If that happens, the guys might get together and put some balls in holes.

Viktor approaches me. "Blake, you look like you're having a good time. Maybe it's that good-looking PA you brought with you."

"Mm, one never knows." I dodge the reference to Rachel. I've forgotten how it is when you're single and not the most popular person in the room.

What have we gotten ourselves into? I was afraid Ashley would manipulate her back into my life. Stupidly, I didn't give myself enough credit to acknowledge that my brain already knew what my heart knew. Now it's as clear as the air I breathe that I was completely over Ashley before we broke up. What possessed me to rope Rachel into posing as my girlfriend?

It's been difficult playing by Rachel's "off-limits" rule she insisted on for us to work together. I've always known it was just a matter of time before that rule was broken. That's how it is when you're an athlete. I'm in the driver's seat, and test drives are awesome. Especially now that I'm single and don't have to answer to anyone other than my team and coaches. I won't do anything stupid that could jeopardize my booming career.

My agent is working on getting Viktor and me a commercial promoting a new vodka brand. I want to buy a house when I know I'll be with a team long enough to settle down.

I can't believe how content I was waking up to Rachel's warm legs wrapped around mine. The last thing I wanted to do was leave the bed or her. If the golf tournament weren't crucial to this trip, I would still be under the bed covers.

As much as we enjoy each other, I don't think she intends to stay in Maine. I bet if her old sponsors got wind of us dating, they would come knocking, and she would let them back in. I get it. Women get sucked into the media attention: the likes, shares, endorsements. When and if that happens, I will pull the ripcord on this no-strings-attached affair because I don't want to live in a social media fishbowl.

Rachel isn't like most girls, but I need to be prepared if things go off the rails. Experience has taught me a glamorous life is filled with enticing mouse traps. I should know. I was stuck in one with Ashley and would have chewed off my foot to get out.

We go straight from the golf course to the clubhouse for a luncheon with the donors. I leave before dessert because Rachel texts me that we have a date with Stevie and Ruth-Ann. I have no fucking clue what she's talking about, and God help me if they're swingers.

I figure Rachel will be at the pool, and she is typing away on her laptop.

"You about done with that?"

Surprised to see me, her face lights up, or did I imagine that?

"Oh, yes, we need to get ready for the fun thing I planned." She collects her stuff, and we walk to the bungalow.

"Really? What is it?" I ask, taking the laptop bag off her shoulder and handing her a chilled water bottle.

"You'll find out," she teases. "Thanks for the water. I need to drink more than just champagne and tequila."

"You're being rather mysterious, little Writer Gal."

Seeing her chin go up and her back straighten, I take the change in posture as an indication she likes the new nickname.

"Writer Gal, eh?"

"I think it's appropriate." I shrug.

She nods and grins, "Yeah, I think so, too," and scrunches up her shoulders in a way that makes me think she's about to skip down the boardwalk in glee.

Rachel suggests we wear sunglasses as we get ready for this mystery outing. I find the suggestion endearing. She's never been outside North America and isn't used to the sun, especially how the brilliant white sand reflects and intensifies the rays.

Rachel mentioned she'd love to travel more, so bringing her with me has inspired her adventurous side. She's come up with a bucket list of places to see when she makes it big.

What if she were to become a best-selling author? Would she want a life in the States or be home in Canada with her family?

Halfway to the beach, she has us detour down a dirt road

where we find a barn and stables. Three horses are saddled up next to a wood fence, and we're greeted by our guide, who introduces us to Stevie and RuthAnn.

"Horses? Really? You couldn't pick something mellow like snorkeling?"

"Where's the fun in looking at fish when you can climb on the back of a horse? I know hockey players, and you're not happy unless an element of danger is involved," she jests, but she's right. We're all adrenaline junkies.

"What if I hurt my wrists? I need everything I have."

"You've got boutique insurance for every inch of you."

"You told me you know nothing about hockey players," I jeer.

"I'm learning daily, trust me. Besides, I've had some time to think about it, and the only difference between you and my brother is that he's older. Other than that, you two are cut from the same cloth."

"I can't wait to meet him."

"Yeah, he's getting home today. He would have loved it here. I've been having so much fun and slept in this morning. I think the sun is tiring me out."

I want to suggest it's all the sex, but I don't want to sound crude. I wonder how she puts up with a hockey-playing brother because we can be downright awful when it comes to the stuff we say and the pranks we play.

We mount and head back down the dirt road toward the beach. By this time of the day, all the tourists have left, and it's just us and the horses.

"Ah, so you're glad you came?" I ask while admiring the view.

"Yes, thanks."

We don't have to do much with the horses. They know to follow the guide on the lead horse so we can relax and enjoy the scenery as the sun comes and goes behind the late afternoon clouds.

The color of the ocean reminds me of that blue curaçao liquor, and I could use a frosty beverage right about now. There's a strawberry margarita machine at the pool bar, but I'm convinced there's more sugar than alcohol in the frozen concoction. But the tourists that flock here from the cruise ships don't seem to mind. It could be frozen cat piss but stick an umbrella in it, and they'll drink it.

This reminds me that I need to hire a dietician, stat. I forgot to take care of it before we left Maine. Rachel sent me the list, and I never bothered to look at it.

We're having a nice relaxing ride along the shoreline when, suddenly, all hell breaks loose. Rachel's horse gets spooked by a rogue wave and bolts past the guide, catching him asleep at the wheel.

I kick my horse into gear, as does our guide, but I have a head start and get to her first. I'm good with horses, having grown up on a farm, and my best friend had a barn full of them.

"Rachel." I yell, "Pull back on the reigns."

She does, but the horse is not having it and goes faster.

"Hang on to the horn on the saddle," I instruct her as I lean over, taking the reins from her hands.

She does as I say.

I give the reins a good yank, and both horses slow to a stop.

Rachel is shaking, her eyes fixed straight ahead.

"I had no idea that could happen."

I dismount and help her off the horse, wrapping my arms around her as our guide holds the reins.

"Are you okay? We have to go back and get ready for the Gala tonight."

"Yeah," she replies, but her head is still buried in my chest.

"You sure? You're a Writer Gal, not a rider gal, eh?"

She finally lifts her head, giggling at my corny joke.

"Yeah, that was a good one. I'm getting hungry, too. Let's go back."

I'm impressed when she returns on her horse, and we ride to the stables with no further incidents.

The conference rooms on the hotel's second floor have been combined to provide as much space as possible for a silent auction fundraiser. We walk around, checking out the items available to bid on, finding table after table of sports memorabilia, most of it signed. I'm not famous enough for my signature to bring big bucks, but I carry one of my hockey sticks.

I smile when I see a framed photo of Finn and read that he's auctioning himself off. The highest bidder will get to play golf with him tomorrow. I should bid just to fuck with him.

Rachel is quiet and patient as I shake hands with the guests who have come to support the Make a Kid Smile program.

"You going to carry that stick all night?" she teases, looking taller tonight in her Jimmy Choo stilettos. I'd love to know what she's wearing under her sexy black cocktail dress.

"Nope, ah ha, there's the person I'm looking for," I say, directing Rachel towards a woman I introduce as Mrs. Gianacola. She shakes Rachel's hand and asks us to follow her.

Rachel gives me a quizzical look. This stop wasn't on the itinerary. I was going to slip away and do this privately, but now that she's here, I'm glad to have her support. I've never done this before and don't know what to expect.

Mrs. Gianacola leads us into a room occupied by a mother and her little girl. The child is in a wheelchair and has no hair.

"Hi, you must be Hannah," I say, shaking her thin hand. She's abnormally frail and pale.

"Yes." She grins, showing her missing front teeth.

"I'm Blake Gibson. This is my friend Rachel."

"Hi, Blake." She looks at Rachel. "I love your dress."

"Oh, thank you," Rachel replies.

Sitting on the corner of the bed, I pull out my marker and sign the stick.

"I understand I'm your favorite hockey player, but now that I'm with the Maulers, are you still going to watch the games?"

"You bet." She beams, cheering up.

"I hear you and your mom got here on a cruise out of Texas."

"Yeah, we used to live in California, but the hospital in Texas was better for me, so we moved there."

"Nice. Do you like it there?"

"Yeah, it's okay."

Her mother asks to take a picture of us, so I kneel beside her wheelchair and put my arm around her shoulder. We both say 'cheese' while her mother takes photos with her cell phone.

Afterward, I get up and ask if she has any questions.

"How did you get so tall?"

I chuckle. "Just born that way. My daddy is tall."

She nods.

"Did you have a good time on your cruise here?"

"Oh, yes, I can't do much, but I love the pool on the ship. And they have shows and a game room."

"Awesome."

She nods.

"I have to go, but it was great meeting you." I lean down and hug her.

Her mother thanks me profusely, and we leave.

"Wow, a heads up would have been nice. That was not on your calendar."

"I know, I wasn't sure how it was going to go, and I didn't know you when the plans were made. She's going through cancer treatments."

"I thought so, sweet kid, very nice. Cancer sucks."

"Yes, it does. I'm glad the cruise made her light up."

"Yeah, she likes it. Good for her. It must be hard to get out and get around."

"Yeah. Let's hope Hannah gets better."

Walking back to the elevator, we're quiet and alone with our thoughts. It's as if someone pulled the plug on our party by taking everything for granted.

We rejoin the gala, and I try my best to act happy, but inside, part of me thinks I'm a prick for not getting more involved with kids who have a lot less than I did growing up.

20

RACHEL

W e're on the way to our room when I get a text from Alexandre. They're home from their honeymoon, and everything is fine. He asks about my trip and tells me I better not be fucking the new guy.

Oh, boy. He's starting his high school, big brother protective shit again.

"What's up?" Blake asks when he sees me looking at my phone.

Damn, he has a sixth sense when it comes to any change in my mood.

"My brother is home."

"Good, everything okay?"

"Yeah, except he thinks he has to protect me from you."

"Oh, no. Is that gonna be an issue?"

"He's made it an issue since high school. Back then, he was a major cockblocker, and I had no clue he was telling his friends and teammates to stay away from me. They treated me like I had the plague, so I thought there was something wrong with me when none of them asked me out."

"That's not cool." The concern in his eyes precedes his frown.

"No, it is not. I cried and thought no one wanted me."

"I hope you kicked his ass for it," he says as we enter the bungalow.

"As if," I reply, rolling my eyes. "Tonight was fun." I change the subject.

I'd love to have another one of his hugs, like the one at the beach after the runaway horse incident. The way he protected me from being hurt can't be denied. However, I wish to experience the safety in his arms again, I don't know where we stand, and the last thing I want to do is come across as clingy.

"We're meeting the guys at the airport early, so we'd better get some rest," he says, heading to his room.

My heart sinks. Is that it? Is it over?

"Are you coming?" floats through the air and wraps around my ears like a snug blanket as my heart leaps.

I look up to see him standing near the pool, with my shoes in his large hand, waiting for me.

"Um, yes, let me just call Charlotte, then I'll be right there."

"Take your time."

I could burst. I want to jump and shout, 'he wants me!' but I have to check in with Charlotte. When I tried earlier, she was busy.

"Charlotte!"

"What?" She's happy to hear from me. Being with Blake has given me a new fondness for Charlotte and the healthy sex life she's maintained in her mid-thirties.

"The charity event was great. The food—was amazing. Did you get the picture of Blake and me at the Gala?"

"Yes, you two look amazing. And, OMG, those shoes.

Jesus, you could sell those and pay two months' rent with the proceeds," she jests.

"Very funny. By the way, Alexandre and Callie are home from Hawaii. You know, he goes to these charity fundraisers every year. I can't believe he never invited me to any of them."

"Rachel, let me remind you, he's never been the most caring of siblings. You have selective memory and forget he was always an ass to you like he was to everyone else. He only cared about himself until he met Callie, so don't beat yourself up. Not to change the subject, but how is the book progressing?"

"Almost done. I wrote all morning, and I'm getting my process down."

"Yeah, normally it takes a while to figure things out, and each book will be better than the last. I have faith in you. The stuff you sent me has been perfect for the market."

"Right, great." I have a more important question. "What do you think Blake will do when we leave here? We've been banging all night, every night, like a couple of honeymooners."

"You'll have to see where it goes, but remember, these professional athletes pick up girls all the time, so don't cry in your pre-made salad if it ends before the jet engines cool in Maine."

"That's easy. This is the warmest time of the year," I joke to cover my fear of rejection.

"You had fun?"

"Loads of it."

"Great, then file this away as a vacation fling. Keep the good memories, and don't get attached. I know you've never really been in love except for your first boyfriend, but he doesn't count. It was college and lasted all of five months."

Is she trying to give me a pep talk? This sounds more like an episode of *This is Your Life,* and mine sucked.

"Just saying, gotta go, my show is on."

"Okay, bye."

I take off my dress and pack it along with almost everything in the room that's mine before heading over to Blake's room.

When he sees me, he turns off the TV and flips the sheets back, inviting me to get in.

He holds me, and we discuss the day as I cuddle in his chiseled arms. He pulls me close and nuzzles my neck before he gives me a sweet kiss, and we fall asleep.

The next thing I know, Blake is standing before me with a coffee cup in his hand.

I sit up. "What time is it?"

"Five, you fell asleep as soon as your head hit my chest. The plan is to meet the guys in the lobby and ride to the airport together. You have one hour to get ready."

I sip the dark brew, watching him pack. He's an efficiency expert, and I remember how much these guys travel.

When I've temporarily filled my memory watching him, I figure I should leave before being labeled a stalker. I slip out of bed, grab his white dress shirt from last night, and use it to cover myself.

Like watching an exotic animal in its natural habitat, this may be my last opportunity to observe him in the same room as me, and he's only wearing his boxer underwear. Who knows what will happen when we step out the door? I'm savoring every minute, having no confidence in there being an "us." This was a no-strings-attached agreement.

I doubt his teammates will make a big deal about us hooking up on the trip. I scanned the area at the gala, and all the guys were hanging out with plenty of women. It seems these men always mix business with pleasure. Even James had a cute girl on his arm last night.

"I forgot to ask how your golf game went yesterday," I ask as I pass by him.

"Oh." He pauses and looks at me as I lean against my door frame, wearing only his dress shirt. I'm still grasping it closed over my chest as I stand self-conscience about being butt naked first thing in the morning.

"It was fine. I had a decent game, but the retired pro golfers did much better."

"Figures. Sorry about that. I'll get dressed."

I put his shirt in my luggage, and if I forget to give it back, it's a great keepsake from the weekend. I wear jeans and a thin beige cashmere top that's comfy.

Blake waits for me at the exit and takes my bag like a gentleman. We meet the guys in the hotel lobby and pile into a van heading to the airport. Nobody is saying much, and they all look half asleep, so it's safe to assume they partied until the wee hours of the morning, enjoying their last day of absolute freedom.

The guys go through the line first and head down the tiny hallway to the plane. But when I hand my passport to the immigration officer, he takes one look at my Canadian passport, assuming he'll give it a cursory glance, stamp it, and let me through. Instead, he calls a supervisor over, and they speak in French to me.

"What? What do you mean I can't leave?" It's not the same French we speak in Quebec, but I got the message.

Thankfully, Blake is behind me when this happens.

"What's up?" he asks.

"He's asking for paperwork I don't have. I didn't know I needed a special visa to return to the States. He's saying I can only fly to Canada," my voice breaks at the end of the sentence, and panic ensues.

This cannot be happening. There goes my job if I even have one after this weekend. My brother will be annoyed, and my poor parents will worry if I'm here alone. I'm worried about being here alone, not to mention the cost involved. I can't even afford coffee here.

Shit, shit, shit.

My parents have enough on their plate with the new grandbaby on the way. I'm an adult, yet my life is a cluster fuck, again.

I'm embarrassed beyond belief. How could I have missed this?

"You've never been out of North America," Blake reasons, "it's an honest mistake. We'll straighten it out and catch a commercial flight later."

"Okay." His reasoning keeps me calm. Inside, my brain knows this is a colossal fuck up. Immigration departs are always a fickle bitch. In my opinion, it's worse than having a meeting with a tax attorney after your return has been flagged.

Blake waves the guys on, telling them we'll catch up to them later. Viktor shrugs but gives the thumbs up, and they're gone.

We need to go into the city and speak to someone at the consulate office.

"Blake, the office isn't open today, it's Sunday. We have to speak to an attorney or wait for the Canadian consulate to open on Monday, and you have to be at training camp on Tuesday."

"We're cutting it close," he agrees.

"You should have gone with the guys."

"Let's find an attorney who will speak to us. Maybe money will open some doors on a Sunday."

We take our luggage with us, not knowing our actual departure day and time. It will undoubtedly mean another night on the island, making it a close call getting home in time for Blake's training day. This is one hell of a crapshoot.

I frantically search the Internet for immigration lawyers while we take a cab into the city.

I'm staring out the window in complete shock and extreme embarrassment. Blake is quiet. I can't bring myself to look at him.

"OMG, this is my mess, not yours." I let out a sigh.

"We'll see what the attorney has to say and go from there. Okay?"

"Sure." I agree, although I'm not convinced this is going to come to the immediate resolution we need. I've read about Canadians getting stuck in foreign countries over weird shit all my life. And now I'm one of them.

I should have known better. I haven't been in the States very long, and my working visa probably isn't showing up in their system here. I haven't received a paycheck and wonder how long I'll be stranded on this island.

I'm ready to freak the fuck out by the time we pull up in front of a red brick building and walk to an office with the words Immigration Law on the door, written in both French and English.

I speak to the receptionist in French, but she has trouble with my Quebec French, so I switch to English. Plus, Blake can follow what's going on at the same time.

It's nearly noon by the time we sit in front of the attorney and explain my situation.

His first words are, "I'm sorry, Ms. Holloway, your situation is futile. The quickest way to get into the US is to marry an American. Once you're back in Maine, you must fix your visa issues and make everything legal.

I turn to Blake. He looks at me, and it's a toss-up as to whose face looks more alarmed.

"You go home. You have to be there. It's your career. I'll be fine. It will take time; my brother can wire me money, and it will eventually get sorted out."

Blake stands and asks me to step outside so we can speak in the hallway.

"Rachel, I can't leave you. My mother left me when I was a teenager. I know what it's like to be left behind. I understand your history with your family and why you've got this complex that you don't matter to anyone. But your safety matters to me. Shit happens to all of us, trust me. But I can't leave you in a foreign country and not know what you're doing, if you have a place to stay, and that someone isn't going to steal you off the street. It's not safe. You've never traveled by yourself other than from airport to airport."

Blake makes a lot of valid points. I've lived a sheltered existence and have zero street skills. He knows I could easily be the victim of human trafficking or killed before I sense I'm in danger.

What would Alexandre do in this situation? He's traveled all over.

But if I call him, it proves I cannot take care of myself.

"Let's get married," Blake blurts out. "It's the only way to get you to the States. No one has to know. We'll keep it quiet and undo it later. It's the favor I owe you for helping with Ashley."

I'm sure he's trying to make me feel better about my colossal mistake, but isn't marrying a hot hockey star a mistake? Wait, this is only for appearances, just another lie to add to the ever-growing list of lies.

It doesn't matter if it solves my current dilemma, gets me into the States, and gets Blake back by training day. It's a win-win. It's only more paperwork, and no one has to know.

"Okay, but only because I can't let everyone down. We'll keep it quiet; I'll live with my brother, and we'll continue working together. Then, after all the visa paperwork is sorted out, we'll undo the marriage."

Blake smiles. "See, you have it all worked out. Whatever you want. It's all temporary. Let's go back inside and find out what the attorney can do to expedite this so we can leave tomorrow."

In the end, the lawyer agreed to take care of all the paperwork and said we should be able to get married tomorrow. Blake books a commercial flight going home tomorrow night to make sure we have enough time.

Crisis averted, right?

21

BLAKE

We head into the capital of Gustavia, where we will spend the night. Our flights for tomorrow are booked, so we are staying at a hotel near the airport. And like everything on the island, it exceeds my expectations with the breathtaking view from the second-floor balcony. Rachel steps onto the balcony to take a deep breath, and I join her, wrapping my arms around her curvy body and kissing her shoulder. I assure her we'll be fine.

I need to make sure tomorrow goes off without a hitch.

After we have lunch on the beach, I tell Rachel to relax by the pool while I run some errands. I know she's dying to ask what I'm up to, but she's too polite to ask me.

First stop, a boutique to buy her a dress. Getting married in a black cocktail dress has bad fucking luck written all over it. Players are, by nature, superstitious, but nothing could be worse than black on your wedding day, even a marriage of convenience.

The saleswoman helped me pick out a size six white dress, simple but elegant. It has short sleeves and some beading and will cling to her cute, curvy bottom. To avoid wrinkles, the saleswoman leaves the dress on a hanger, covers it with a plastic bag as the dry cleaner uses, and slips it into a cloth carry-on.

Next stop, a jewelry store where I know everything will be overpriced to take advantage of the rich and famous who come to these islands and rent huge homes overlooking the water for their private beach getaways.

It's the price I pay for the ability to get what I want when I want it. And right now, I don't have a lot of options because this island is roughly ten miles long.

The things I'm willing to do to make Rachel see how special she is. She's a great human being, and it's a shame she's always lived in her brother's shadow. I have no idea what that's like. My brother and I both play sports and are closer than most siblings because there were only men in the house growing up.

Rachel's work on her book requires creativity and a lot of nerve. It cannot be easy to put herself out there in print for others to critique and comment on, let alone how hard she's been working on it. Her BFF, Charlotte, is a copywriter and is supposed to have some contacts, but it's not likely she will land an agent who can publish and promote her book.

Her type of agent is more difficult to come by than mine. I'll cross that bridge later. First things first. And right now, all I want is for her to be the center of the universe on her wedding day so we can get home tomorrow night because my ass is grass if I'm not in training camp Tuesday morning.

A tiny bell on the door jingles as I enter the jewelry store. I tell the owner what I'm looking for, and he brings out trays of diamond rings. I guess her ring size, given how petite she is.

This is the first time I've ever purchased a ring and the first time I ever met a woman who drives me wild with all these pent-up emotions. I am obsessed with her and haven't looked twice at another woman since I watched her pull her luggage into the house next door.

The boob slip, that was hysterical. She was so embarrassed then, but I liked how she blushed and covered herself up while continuing to talk to me. She gets points for not running away because of a wardrobe malfunction.

You can't be with a hockey player unless you have a raunchy sense of humor and can hang out with a rough bunch —we chew tobacco, spit everywhere, and say tons of inappropriate, insensitive things to each other. Sometimes, those hurtful comments are directed at people outside our hockey circle, and that's when players can get fired, but overall, we're human.

We can drink too much occasionally, as life on the road is lonely. Some couples have understandings that allow the man to cheat when he's on the road, but I'm not one of those guys. So, this fake marriage better include lots of fucking.

The shopkeeper brings out another tray of rings, and I find the perfect one. The setting is traditional, with rows of brilliant diamonds surrounding a three-carat round diamond with smaller ones around it. Something about this ring speaks to me. I've overheard women saying that, and until today, I'd dismiss the ability of an inanimate object to speak to anyone.

I fork over my credit card with the highest limit and put the small, felt-lined box in my pocket. Now it's time I track down the mayor of this place because I'm leaving nothing to chance. We're both getting home tomorrow, come hell or high water. They better not try to stop me or piss me off. I have a reputation for being difficult when I get really pissed.

I ask around and tip well to find out where the mayor lives. I should have known he'd have the only mansion at the end of the main street, the one with the columns out front like the plantations in Georgia.

I knock on the door. I wait. I knock again.

A woman wearing an apron answers. "Yes, sir. May I help you?"

"I'm looking for Mayor Blanchard. Is he around?"

"It's Sunday, sir."

"It's extremely important. I'm a professional athlete. I happen to be in the area, and I think we may be able to help each other."

"Let me check." Her English has a French lilt to it.

As I'm waiting, a dress slung over my shoulder and a ring in my pocket, it occurs to me I should have started with the mayor.

My thoughts are interrupted by an older gentleman coming to the door. We introduce ourselves, then he invites me in, and I follow him to the backyard, where we sit in the shade, and the housekeeper brings us lemonade. We talked, and over the course of the conversation, I offered to make a commercial-free of charge for his tourism project if he would marry us and bend a few rules.

He agrees, and we shake hands to seal the deal, and I leave with a smile on my face.

Back at the hotel, I find Rachel in her sweet, white bikini, sitting under an umbrella at the beach, typing away. She's dedicated to that book. But thinking back over the past week, she's committed to every project she takes on.

This shouldn't surprise me; she's lived her entire life trying to measure up to her brother, and I can see where her success at being an influencer might have alleviated some of the deficit she's experienced over the years. It's the logical assumption, given the fact we've gotten to know each other much better since our first hookup in the country bar.

I can't believe I'm about to do what I have planned, but everything must be done correctly. That's how a person gets ahead in life. I'm weird that way. Some things must be done perfectly.

I wouldn't be where I am if I didn't pursue perfection like Rachel. We're both in competitive professions and are pressured to improve continually; her with each keystroke and me with each play on the ice.

A wedding can't happen without a proposal.

I lay the dress on a lounger next to hers, and she looks up.

"Everything okay? Oh, please tell me we can go home tomorrow," she exclaims. Her eyes looked a bit puffy, and I wouldn't put it past her to have a good cry. I'm sure she considers herself a burden to her family and now—me.

"I met with the mayor and promised him I'd appear in a commercial to encourage tourism. It's not like he really needs it, but negotiations go better if you make it look like you have something to offer. He said to text him the marriage application information. When we show up tomorrow with our passports, he'll make sure we can leave as scheduled."

Rachel sets her laptop down and leaps out of the chair, throwing her arms around my neck. Then she starts dancing in the white sand and chanting, "Yes, yes, yes. I get to go home."

I like the way home sounds coming from her sweet lips. The smile on her face has me pulling out my phone to capture this special moment, taking pictures of her and selfies of the two of us on the beach.

"And there's more."

"More? More what?"

I drop to one knee. "Rachel Holloway, will you fake marry me?"

She giggles until I open the box, and her hands fly to her face to cover her surprised look.

"Oh, Blake." She eyes the fancy box. It's registering to her that it's not a fake. "This is way too expensive, especially here. We don't need a ring."

This is her putting herself last again, and I won't stand for it.

"Nope, there is no way a wedding should take place without a ring. You can take it off at home to hide the fact that we're married, but until then, it's out of this box."

"Okay."

"Is that a yes, Rachel?"

"Yes, I'll fake wed you, Blake Gibson." She smiles. I take her hand and slide the ring on her finger, and it fits perfectly.

"Oh, my. Charlotte is going to have a heart attack."

I know she's her best friend but fuck, things have a way of getting around. A secret is only a secret if no one knows. I've been on teams my entire life, and one thing is true of women, few can keep a secret. They say something, then it spills over into the locker room. It's not like men don't have the same inclination. Guys can pass around secrets like joints at a reggae concert.

We hug, and I drop a quick kiss on her lips as if to seal the deal, wondering how long it will take for this to blow up on us. I allow myself a few minutes to enjoy how happy she is, and I'm satisfied that the ring on her finger will not pale next to the other wives' should she need to wear it. Her ring is kissed by the tropical sun, and it casts different colors against the ocean backdrop.

This wedding is our ticket home, and I'm gaining confidence that I'll make it to training camp on time.

"What's in the bag?" She eyes the only other gift that isn't inside my jeans and hasn't been unwrapped.

"Oh, I picked up a dress for you. I hope it fits. I had to bribe the shopkeeper to open her shop for me on a Sunday. There is no way in hell you are getting married in a black dress. It's a superstition," I explain.

"Don't I know," she chuckles. "Alexandre didn't wash his socks as long as the team was winning in high school. They were undefeated for months. Those socks stunk up the car so bad I prayed for one loss just so he'd let Mom wash them," she scoffs.

"Right, so getting married in your black dress—bad idea."

"Oh, right. I was so upset I didn't even think about it, but you told me to stay here."

"I did, so I took care of everything."

She squeals and throws her arms around my neck. We have a quick kiss just because we're happy things are going our way, but it turns into a deeper kiss, and it's so natural guests walking by would think we've been together forever. At the least, we resemble the affection and energy of newlyweds.

"Let's get something to eat. I'm hungry," I announce, feeling the rumble in my stomach.

"Let me grab my stuff." She leans over, and I see her ass begging to be smacked, but we're in public, so I settle for admiring the view. There will be time for that later.

Back in our room, she changes into a sundress that's not skintight, and I still find her sexy. She's appealing to my libido no matter what she's wearing. She walks towards me with a narrow box in her hand, which she hands to me.

"You weren't to leave the hotel."

"I know, it's a little something."

It's a tie box and designer. She must have gotten it at the hotel gift shop.

"A blue tie," I lift it from the box. It's imported from

France, and she paid too much for it, but I love it. The paisley print matches the colors of the island waters, and I've never seen one quite like it.

"I guess you'll have to be my something borrowed and something blue," she quips.

"I'm borrowed?" Questioning her meaning, my eyebrows furrow, and my lips grin.

"Well, fake husband and all. . ."

"Oh, I get it." That's clever. See, she's the creative one. I'm not a big reader, but I'd love to know what she's writing in her book.

I admit she's a bit of an enigma, but I'm up to the challenge of figuring her out.

And we both love the challenge of a large bed that feels small when we fuck each other all over it. It's like traveling the world in four hours when the bedsheets are skewed, the blankets are on the floor, and sometimes the pillows sail through the air.

She thinks we need to pick up the room. I informed her that's what maid service is for, and it's called a vacation for a reason. She blushed.

Now, to find some incredibly expensive French cuisine and to pop some champagne. It might be a fake wedding, but I'm a stickler for protocols and intend to do this right. I've started celebrations over less important things at noon, but Rachel deserves the best. I'm happy I can make this her dream vacation and get us both home in time. With lady luck on our side, our plan will go off without a hitch. The pun is intended.

I chuckle, I'm getting hitched, and it's not as terrible as I thought.

22

RACHEL

I can't believe Blake and all he's doing. I'm blown away by all the thought he put into tomorrow. It will make it so damn difficult when we get back home and go back to our professional relationship.

Damn, why did I have to do something so stupid? Passports and visas are not my strong suit.

Ugg. If my brother finds out about this, I will never live it down.

I'm hiding in the bathroom, texting Charlotte.

We're getting fake married so I can return to the States. Don't tell anyone because no one can know. Everything will stay the same as it was before the trip.

You mean the trip with the most incredible sex of your life, according to what you're writing. I don't need to speak to you to see what's going on here. You guys have the hots for each other.

No, we don't, we're just fucking around. You know, no strings attached. Grown up to grown up.

Sure, and donkeys fly.

Dumbo does, oh, yeah, he was an elephant. Fuck.

Right. I told you to be careful. DO NOT FALL FOR HIM.

No need to scream at me, but I read you loud and clear. I love you, Char.

Love you, kid.

Now, one person knows what's going on in my life. I wish she was here. Damn. But the wedding isn't real anyway, so it's no biggie. What the hell do I have to lose?

I find Blake on the balcony texting on his phone. I feel a twinge of jealousy. What if he's talking to a girl, the new girl, the next girl, right now? To my horror, that's all I can think about.

Fair is fair. I could have been texting a guy in the bathroom. Maybe he needs to talk to someone, too.

But I know Ashley is still on the island. She's here for a week.

I look at the shiny bling on my ring finger. Does it really mean something, or are we still on island time?

"It's getting late; how about dinner on the beach patio?" Blake asks, coming in from the balcony along with the salty wind that blows the sheers hanging from the door.

"Great." I perk up at the thought of us doing something together, but inside, I blame myself for this mess. I'm costing him time and money, and if the plane is delayed, he's screwed. And not in the way he'd like it. I should know after being turned upside down, sideways, and everything in between every night. One thing I can say from experience is these boys have stamina.

"Look, I just want to say I'm so sorry for all this. If you want to go home tonight, I'm fine. I'm sure I'll be okay." I fold my hands in front of me like an innocent schoolgirl, nervous as hell.

"What? It's not a big deal." He flips his phone to the screensaver. It's a picture of him making a goal in a game. "I just let my agent know I'll make training camp Tuesday in case of—y'know, anything delays the plane."

"Right, I didn't mean to pry. . ."

"You didn't. I'm just filling you in. We have to look like we're getting married for the right reason or else the feds could make your life miserable. It has to look legit tomorrow because it will take longer to undo if we're exposed. You understand that, right?"

"Yeahhh. . ." However, I can't shake the feeling I'm constantly being a burden to those I love, and now him.

He approaches me and lifts my chin, forcing me to look into his drop-dead, dreamy eyes.

Fuck me, I can never say 'no' to him. Nor can I hide my thoughts from him, and panic sets in. I want to escape. I'm overwhelmed— the situation, the wedding. I can't breathe.

Is this what letting someone in does to a person? I'm like a helpless, bleating baby lamb in his arms. When did that happen?

"There is a potentially serious side to this, that's all," he says as his hand falls away.

I take a deep breath, pushing the anxiety down in my chest, which feels full already.

~

The dress Blake picked out for me fits perfectly. After he zips me into it, we walk hand in hand, picking up fresh flowers along the way—nothing like a fresh bouquet for the bride.

After meeting the mayor and his wife at their beautiful home, we follow them to the backyard. Blake props up his phone on a table, and the well-known song "A Thousand

Years" starts playing. I cannot listen to that song without getting goosebumps and tearing up. How did he know?

While the song plays in the background, Mayor Blanchard insists on walking me down the brick walkway toward the makeshift altar. I can't take my eyes off Blake, waiting for me under a huge tree dripping with orchids in every color.

The mayor's wife, our witness, joins us under a pergola covered with pink bougainvillea flowers.

The song ends, and so do my tears. It's a good thing because my waterproof mascara is being tested like never before. If I'm asked, I will give it a great review because, in my opinion, it has outperformed.

Perhaps my tears are because I secretly wish this was all real, a real husband, a real marriage, and not just a façade. The dating scene is a rat race with more rats and traps than cheese. When and if you do find 'the one,' how are you to snag him? I can't compete with the women who hang around these athletes, and I don't belong in this world.

Mayor Blanchard does an excellent job with the vows and declares us man and wife. Blake and I kiss, thank the mayor, say our goodbyes, and take a leisurely stroll through town with our papers. People on the street are friendly and congratulate us, and it feels real.

That's the thing, it feels natural. The flowers, the song, the dress. Blake's more romantic than Rhett Butler, pursuing Scarlett, even though she never appreciated him.

How can I show Blake I appreciate him? I can't thank him enough. We swing by our hotel to change into more comfortable clothes before heading to the airport. This time, we have no problems passing through immigration and boarding a flight to the US.

Our connection is in South Carolina, so we take the opportunity to eat southern BBQ in between flights. Blake excuses himself to take a phone call and walks away from the table.

He returns, and we head to our gate, where we sit charging our phones. I work on my book, and Blake plays on his phone.

"How's the book going, Writer Gal, eh?"

"I think it's appropriate." I shrug.

I smile, and like that he has a nickname for me.

"Good. I should have it finished this week. Then, I'll send it to Charlotte for final edits and see what happens next."

"That's awesome. I can't imagine how I'd feel putting something like that out for the world to see and judge. I'm proud of you," he says, leaning over and kissing my forehead.

I'm focused on the small screen before me, but I put my hand on his leg and give it a slight squeeze to thank him, an innocuous return of the sentiment.

"I don't know how you do what you do either. I tried figure skating when I was little, tried being the operative word."

He chuckles as I start to type. "I get that. Figure skating is different. Maybe you should have tried hockey."

To which I let out a huge *Pfft*. Like I'd be able to do anything better than my brother.

He chuckles again. "Oh, look, we're getting ready to board."

I inhale deeply and let it out slowly before packing up.

Blake takes my carry-on bag like a gentleman. I'm still overwhelmed by the day and can't believe we did what we did. On top of it, Blake got us matching wedding bands, and the set on my finger would make any woman envious.

"Should we take our rings off?" I whisper to him.

"Let's wait until we get home so we don't lose them," he

says, handing the agent our tickets, and we board for the final destination.

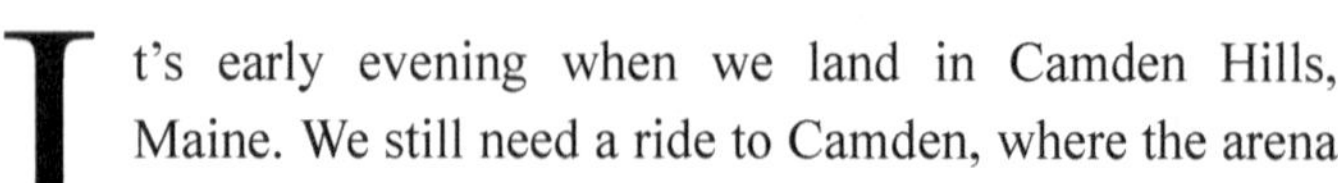

I t's early evening when we land in Camden Hills, Maine. We still need a ride to Camden, where the arena is and our exclusive suburb.

"I can't believe how tiny this airport is and that you guys go everywhere from here—except overseas."

"Maybe we'll make an All-Star game. Who knows? But it's nice here. I don't miss the LA traffic, and I don't miss the beach as much as I thought I would. The traffic is so bad it has to be a big deal for friends to get together for it to be worth the hassle."

"Hmm. I wouldn't know. I always lived in a landlocked territory." I smile as we walk past that infamous moose that scared the shit out of me my first time here.

The airport is quiet as we wait for our luggage, but when I look out the exit doors that open automatically, hundreds of people are standing there. Even for Maine, this is unusual.

I assume this is all because Blake Gibson, the local hockey star, is home, and some fans are here to welcome him. Blake isn't fazed by much, and he grabs our bags and turns. We walk through the doors, not suspecting anything out of the ordinary, but as soon as the cool evening air hits my face, so does the light of flashbulbs. To make matters worse, everyone in the crowd is shouting questions.

Did someone ask if we're married?

23

BLAKE

To say I'm unprepared for the mob scene at the airport is putting it mildly. It's the understatement of the 21st century.

Shock and awes, like what I'd witness in a fighter movie, come to mind when flash photography goes off in our faces as soon as we step outside. I planned to take a taxi, but I can't get to the taxi stand, and who knows if even one is available. The reporters push in closer, making me uncomfortable. This could escalate and get out of hand quickly.

"Is it true you got married on St. Bart's'?" I hear someone shout.

"How long have you been seeing Rachel?" Another voice in the crowd shouts.

"Yeah, we want to know how you two met," chimes in someone else.

"What happened with Ashley?"

Fuck that question. Really? This is the best the media can come up with? No congratulations; I hope you had a nice time. . . nothing.

Rachel and I turn to each other simultaneously. Our eyes lock, and I can tell she's putting on a brave face.

"What do we do?" she mouths.

I feel the platinum wedding band on my finger that matches her ring and rub my thumb over its smoothness. I crack a smile, recalling how gorgeous Rachel looked walking towards me, how my chest swelled with pride and the desire to take care of her. I could blame everything on the salt air, the incredible sex, and being 'marooned' on the island for three days. There is a reason it's a honeymoon destination for the rich and famous.

"We're tired, guys. I'll make a statement later. Right now, we want to get home," is my only comment as I push through the media circus, keeping Rachel tucked safely under my arm.

A car pulls up to us out of nowhere, and then Rachel yells, "Yeah. That's Callie's car." Rachel's brother hops out the passenger side, quickly opens the trunk, and yells at Rachel to get in.

I help Alexandre put the luggage in the trunk.

Rachel is in the back seat, and I slide in next to her, slamming the door in some reporter's face. Alexandre hops in the front passenger seat and says, "Floor it," while still buckling his seatbelt.

Baby, on the way or not, Callie drives like we just robbed a bank, finding the airport exit and getting us on the highway quickly.

"Hi, guys," Callie says with more enthusiasm than I can muster at the moment.

"Thank you so much for rescuing us. How did you know we were going to be mobbed?"

"We thought it was weird when Viktor and Finn returned without you guys and couldn't tell us what happened at the airport. They assumed you two had so much fun you wanted another day. But then. . ."

"It was on the news," Callie blurts out. "It's trending everywhere. The mayor of St. Bart's released a short video of you two getting married, and I must say it was beautiful."

"Oh, really?" Now I know why the mayor was so accommodating. The bastard had this planned all along and took advantage of my situation for free publicity. He had no right to put my private life on blast, and he can forget about me making him a commercial. The deal is off.

"You could sue," Rachel murmurs to me.

"It's fine."

"So," Alexandre turns in his seat, "Hi, brother, nice to meet you." He's flashing me a smile that I can't return.

The corners of my mouth turn slightly, and I nod, but I'm still miffed over the mayor spilling the beans. What does that man not understand about confidentiality? Good thing he didn't know it was fake or that, too, would be splashed all over the tabloids.

"Hi, sorry, we're just tired."

"I bet," Callie adds with a wink, like she's in on the joke and knows we were banging our brains out all weekend. "So, St. Bart's, lucky devil, Rachel."

She changes lanes, and I glance over my shoulder to see a few cars following us. Dammit!

Callie glances in the rearview mirror and notices them, too.

"We didn't get this kind of attention when we returned from our honeymoon. Look at us; we have anniversaries in the same month." Her excitement rings in my ears.

I want to get home and hide under the covers until this blows over. Now my family and friends are going to find out and be rightfully pissed because I never mentioned Rachel to anyone. I look like a real douchebag.

Not to mention that Rachel and I now have to live the lie. This means the time frame on this is infinitely longer than we intended.

I should have never lied, but I thought we'd undo the marriage before anyone found out. We'll have to be extra careful to keep up appearances because we both have too much to lose.

Getting in trouble with immigration won't bode well for the vodka commercial I just landed, an endorsement deal I haven't even shared with Rachel.

I overestimated the good in people, and it's come home to roost.

Shit.

Rachel is too quiet for a newlywed, and I give her a look and a nudge, encouraging her to play it up.

"Yeah, the island worked its magic on us. I mean, the turquoise water, the horseback ride on the beach where Blake had to save me because my horse bolted."

"What?" Alexandre asks, alarmed.

"It's fine. Blake knows horses and saved me before the guide knew what happened."

I turn to see how many cars are following us. I hold up three fingers for Rachel to see.

Whew, maybe they'll back off now that they have their pictures.

"Wow, thanks, Blake," Alexandre quips. "So, my lil' sis is married. Do Mom and Dad know yet?"

"They probably do now. I didn't tell anyone because it all happened so quickly," Rachel replies.

We arrive at our gated community.

"Still a few reporters behind us," I announce.

"I'll drive through the gate and stop until the gate closes so they can't follow us in," Callie confirms and does just that.

The media truck with the satellite dish on top would have to ram her car to get in at this point.

Within minutes, Callie pulls into my driveway and hugs and congratulates Rachel; then, she hugs me.

Alexandre and I grab the luggage. I shake his hand and thank him profusely.

"No problem, man. I got your back," he says, patting me on my shoulder as I turn to help Rachel into the house.

"I thought we'd never get here," Rachel says.

"I know, thankfully, your brother and Callie were on top of this. Fuck that mayor. Thanks to him, we're going to be all the press talks about for weeks," I say, dragging our luggage to my bedroom.

"Spring training starts tomorrow. I'm sure we'll be old news." Rachel is trying to minimize the situation, but I blame myself. I didn't think anyone could create this much heat for us, so I thought we'd fly under the radar.

It's been dark for hours, and I catch Rachel yawning. I never knew leaving the tropics would have me feeling so exhausted. Maybe it's the transition from the humid island air to the dry air of Maine.

"Are you hungry?"

"Guess we should eat something." I look at my phone and see it's after eight.

Rachel's phone dings.

"Ah, it's Callie. She left some dinner in the fridge for us," she says, smiling. "Thank goodness for my wonderful sister-in-law. Now I know that little something she wanted to do to make us feel at home," Rachel adds. "I hope you don't mind, She knew the keyless entry, but she left food when she found out we got married, and the media frenzy started. That's what she told me."

"I'll eat about anything. What is it?" I ask, looking over her shoulder into the fridge.

"A mystery casserole," she teases. I take it from the fridge and transfer it to the microwave. I'm no cook, but I can handle reheating food. Most everything I eat cooks in two minutes or less when I'm alone.

Rachel pulls plates from the cabinets and forks from the silverware drawer.

I dish some of the casseroles onto our plates, and we sit at the table like a couple. I've never lived with a girl, so this feels different, and yet Rachel and I have fallen into a routine like it's nothing.

"This is good. Tuna casserole, I ate a ton of it as a kid."

"Hum, well, we ate a lot of pot pies, but they're different in Canada. Instead of chicken or tuna, we use some of the game we hunt."

"Interesting. I'd like to try that someday. By the way, how's your book going? Does Charlotte like it?"

I'm trying to avoid talking about the fiasco at the airport because I don't know what to do or say about it.

"So, the airport, crazy, eh?"

"Yeah." And it looks like we're going to talk about it. "I'm shocked. The mayor played me."

"I can't tell you how sorry I am about all this."

"We'll figure it out. In the meantime, I guess you're bunking with me, huh?" and I can't hold in a mischievous grin.

"Hmm." She puts her cute pointer finger on her chin as if she's thinking. "No strings attached?"

"Sure. But we have to keep up appearances, so no stepping out on each other. We can undo this once your visa is worked out and things die down."

"Sounds good. Do you have any wine?"

I stand. "Yes, I do," I reply, grabbing two wine glasses and a dry red from the wine rack built into the kitchen cabinet.

"Don't you have training camp first thing in the morning?"

"Yep." I smile.

Fuck if I don't have a boner already. I doubt we'll have time to drink the entire bottle tonight.

24

RACHEL

I enjoy the rearview as I watch Blake walk to the shower. We never made it to the second glass of wine last night. I have no clue what I'm supposed to be doing now that we're fake married, but I do love the feel of his body against mine at night and waking up to see his face on the pillow next to me in the morning.

How can I pretend to care for him and be married when I'm supposed to be distant and unattached emotionally to protect myself? Logically it doesn't make sense, and yet it's my life. Making it look real to the world is a mind-bender, a contradiction not only in terms but also in the fact is we will eventually end our relationship.

"Do I report to my boss today?" I ask when he steps out of the shower to dry himself.

The snide smile on his face tells me he remembers last night. Not that we've had anything but memorable nights together.

"I think a wife can do what I need as she finishes writing her book. I'll give you an allowance; your debit card is probably in the mailbox. Can you go through the mail? Don't forget about the visa issue that needs to be fixed. At this point, that needs to be your priority."

"Yeah, that's going to be a colossal pain in the ass. I hate red tape and paperwork."

"Obviously." He softens the blow with a kiss he plants on my head. "Also, please call the Maulers and see what they need for insurance on you and file our marriage license. I imagine they want an official engagement picture, so we might have to fit that in before I go on the road."

"On it." I type notes into my phone. "Anything else?"

"Please hire a nutritionist for me as soon as possible."

"How do I know what you need?"

"Writer Gal, you always know what I need," he says, disappearing into the walk-in closet, where he dresses in a suit and comes out, putting his tie on as the final touch.

"Mm, the season is about to start, and footage of y'all in suits walking to the arena will pop up everywhere."

"Let's hope it replaces the video of us getting married," he mumbles.

This is the first indication I have that he might not be happy with our arrangement. For all I know, he has many women lined up for the season on the road. But as he said, we have to be on the straight and narrow.

Pretending to be man and wife will keep us both off the market. I brush my doubts away. He offered, and I accepted. I had to be a fake girlfriend to help him with Ashley, and he had to be a fake husband to get me into the States. You can say we're even.

Now, he's allowing me to spend my days writing. The timing is perfect because I've been on a roll, and I'm in my characters' world and don't want to stop writing. I'll see what Charlotte thinks about my progress later.

"Do I cancel my job with the service?"

"Sure, it would look weird otherwise, wouldn't it?"

"I guess so." What changed his normally chipper mood? Training day jitters?

"Okay, I'm going to grab a coffee; I'll see you tonight," he says, leaving me without a kiss goodbye.

"Have a nice day," I sarcastically holler after him and wonder if it's something I said.

I hear the garage door go up and down, and I'm left alone in this humongous house and have no idea what I'm supposed to be doing. I reckon I'll check the mail, see if my card is here, get groceries, and pretend to be a housewife. Oh, and take care of the visa paperwork.

Callie can fill me in on things I need to know. Besides, I need to get what little clothes I have from my room in their house. Now that she's back from vacation, she has Lucy, her sweet dog, in the house.

Charlotte texted.

Girl, told ya, look at you. You're making headlines up here, and I wonder what all the fuss is about. Alexandre is what the Canadians want.

Then my phone rings. It's my mom.

Oh, shit, fuck, damn.

Mom and Dad.

Gotta go. Mom calling. TTYL.

"Hi, Mom, how are you?" I answer as quickly as possible to make sure she doesn't panic.

"What's this, you're married? We never met this man. We didn't even know you were dating anyone. Last we heard, you were going to Maine to work for Alexandre," she exclaims, wildly intent on working herself up over nothing. I stifle a chuckle at her reaction since Blake, and I are fake everything. I don't want her to hear me laughing because we're duping everyone, and that deceit will weigh on me. But until then, I might as well enjoy the short-lived approval of my parents, even if they are confused. I'm sure they see me as a success now.

We've both learned that little lies become larger lies, and we got that in spades at the airport. I could wring the neck of that two-faced mayor.

This is throwing Mom for a loop.

"Mom, you should be happy for me." I shirk the truth.

"I am, dear, but he's not Joel. He's a stranger. We knew Joel."

Ugh. When will that ever die the overdo death it deserves?

"Look, I'm sure you'll meet him soon enough."

"Well, maybe he'll give you a steady life, and you can forget that social media silliness and forget about that book you're trying to write. You need to get a real job and keep your nose to the grindstone. We need to see you settled before we die."

"Oh, Mom, you're not going anywhere. I'm sure we'll see you soon. It all happened so fast, and the press surprised us, so I'm sorry you didn't hear it from me."

"It's fine. I have two famous kids to brag about."

Ha, she thinks I'm famous. It's not the fame I deserve, but I doubt she'd understand the difference. She's from a world where the men make the rules. The proverbial go to college and get married adage.

I'm pushed back into my shell with her as she's still dissing all my attempts at every career I try. I'm sure she's comparing me to my brother again, only now I'm in the spotlight, and she sounds happy with me for a change.

This doesn't stop me from wishing she would understand that women can have successful careers.

I'll thank her later when I make it on my own and not

Blake's plushy coattails. Until then, I take her rhetoric with a grain of salt. I force myself to write, it's for me, but when someone tells me I can't do something, I always prove them wrong. I'll do the same with the book. It's just a matter of time.

"Tell Dad 'hi' for me. I have to go get groceries."

She rings off, and I text Charlotte.

They know. My mom thinks I'm famous. I'll text more later.

Meanwhile, there's no food in the fridge, so I make a list.

On the way to the mailbox, it crosses my mind that my brother and his wife live next door, so there will be very little room not to be a couple. Callie is a numbers person and good at picking up small details.

The mailbox is full of mail that has accumulated since we left. I flip through the envelopes, and eureka, my card is here.

When I go back inside, I see car keys hanging inside the laundry room and open the door that leads to the garage, curious if Blake owns anything other than his sports car.

Walking to the only vehicle here, the old truck, I take a few steps closer to look it over. It's an old red truck, maybe a collectible. I check the plate on the front, and it's a California plate. I looked inside, and it's in good condition, older, with none of the new features. I wonder if it runs.

I don't want to bother Blake on his first day at work, so I open the door, get inside, and crank it up. The engine springs to life and purrs like an industrial air conditioner. I race inside for my card, grocery list, and purse, experiencing high hopes for the day.

Not only do I need to make it to the store and back, I have to figure out what to cook. Charlotte would wet herself at the thought of me cooking, but I'd like to try it.

It feels good not to be alone eating frozen meals in front

of the TV, watching the Hallmark channel, and looking forward to my vibrator. I'm married now, and we have to make it look real. I have no idea what he likes other than steak and potatoes. Who can go wrong with that?

Well, I did go wrong with that and lost my sponsors.

Fuck them.

I grab two huge steaks with confidence and veggies to go with it. I pick up a few more items. I have no idea how much is in my bank account, and I hope it covers the bill as I use my debit card for the first time. It clears, and I'm home in a few minutes.

I text Callie, asking her what time the men get home.

She texts seven and to come over when I can.

I'm sure she wants more details on our affair turned wedding.

I'm not good at lying, so I'm glad Blake put so much detail into our wedding. He must have thought ahead in case this happened. I've only known him briefly, but I think he is a romantic.

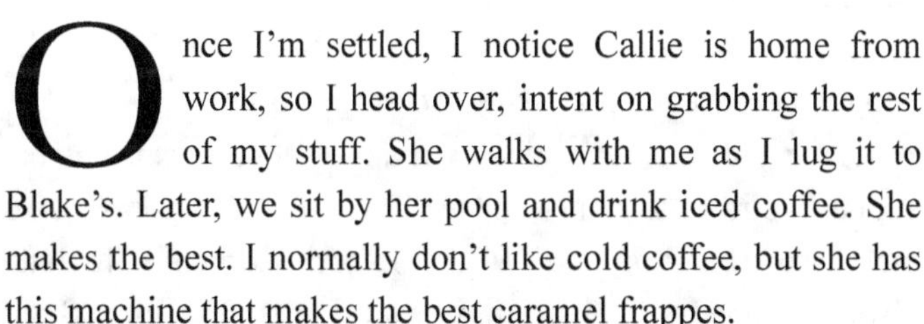

Once I'm settled, I notice Callie is home from work, so I head over, intent on grabbing the rest of my stuff. She walks with me as I lug it to Blake's. Later, we sit by her pool and drink iced coffee. She makes the best. I normally don't like cold coffee, but she has this machine that makes the best caramel frappes.

"Tell me everything," she exclaims, pulling up a chair.

I love Callie. She's a Mainer, born and bred. I love the way she talks. Thankfully, she doesn't sound like the old fishermen and truckers here. Instead, she has a laid-back, relaxed rhythm. Her accent isn't Bostonian or British. It's more like a rough version of the Beatles.

She doesn't pronounce the r's in words, they sound more like h's and b's. I'm not sure, but it's smooth and easy on my ears.

"I had no idea; it was sudden, nice, and dreamy. The island is spectacular in every way."

"I bet." Her eyes widen as she listens. "You look so much more relaxed. I think he's good for you. Your brother played it off, but he will not stop thinking of you as his kid sister."

"Tell me about it," I say, staring at the pool I used to swim in. It's a perfect fall day with no humidity, and I suppose a front of cooler weather is on the way. It's September. The nighttime temps will likely dip into the fifties.

"Tell me about you," I implore her to keep the focus off me. "You got married quickly, and the baby and the honeymoon. You've set a record on how much one woman can accomplish in less than a year."

Callie and I hit it off from the beginning. I'm all for the two of them being together. I don't know if it's because of Alex, the baby, or both, but her face glows. She tells me she wasn't upset with the unplanned pregnancy and that my brother has become a better person. Nothing could make me happier because the play *Wicked* comes to mind.

After coffee with Callie, I returned to my house. That sounds weird to say, 'my house.' There's no room in Blake's closet, so I hang my stuff in the second bedroom. Charlotte always droned on about how weird men can get about change. God forbid I give Blake any indication we're serious. I don't want him avoiding me like poison ivy. Honestly, I doubt he'll want to pass up a night of sex last night because we are sweaty and exhausted. But, the sex intense we discovered this morning the bed sheets were shredded.

I do give myself a drawer in the dresser. It's only fair as I merge his socks and boxers together. Hell, even girlfriends get a panty drawer.

I call my job with the intent to resign, but after I chatted with them about hypotheticals, they warned me they will cancel my work visa if I did not work. After I hung up, I made a note to call the Canadian Embassy later this week. I just love red tape.

When it comes to food prep, I'm only good with salads, so I watch some online videos on how to cook a steak and potatoes. I figure a fake wife should know how to cook more than boxed food. Additionally, I doubt anything coming out of a box is on Blake's approved list of food. In fact, I need to hire a nutritionist and have them make me a list.

I work on my book for a few hours before realizing it's time to make dinner. I hope I don't overcook the steaks. I can't take any more of 'life's most embarrassing' moments in front of Blake.

25

BLAKE

The first day of training is always met with mixed emotions: thoughts of the team I left behind, getting to know new teammates, and figuring out how to play well together on the ice. Of course, there are conditioning regimens to do before we get to that part.

Today began with standard pre-season pep talks and ended with drills. It will take time to warm up to the coaches, but my first day wasn't that bad.

It's stressful being traded. One never knows if the new team will be the same as the last, better or worse. It doesn't matter what I think or feel. What matters is how we play. The coach wants us to excel so we have a winning season. The quest for the cup will start with our first regulation game.

It's the first time I've had a woman at home waiting for me; oddly, I find it comforting. I greet Rachel with a quick kiss as I walk through the door. I'm met with her sheepish-looking eyes peering through her long lashes and the distinct odor of burnt potatoes. Following her into the kitchen, I see that she's cooked steaks, but judging from all the blood on the plate, they're on the raw side of rare. It looks like neither of us spent much time cooking in our single life.

"Wine?" she asks.

"Sure."

I notice the table is set with plates, napkins, and forks. Hmm. This is a thoughtful touch. Rachel pours both glasses of wine and serves the food before joining me at the table.

"Did you find me a nutritionist?"

"I'm working on it. I made some inquiries, and they're not cheap."

"To me, it's a necessary expense to be at the top of my game. Pick someone you can work with. If they don't work out, we'll hire someone else."

"Okay," she says while removing the burnt part of her potato. "Callie and I spent the afternoon together and moved my stuff in. I hope you don't mind."

"Appearances are important," I say, cutting into my steak and half, expecting it to moo.

Rachel puts her knife down. "This steak isn't done."

"I'll throw them on the grill," I suggest, springing up to head outside.

"I'm sorry, I'm not very good in the kitchen." She offers an apology that drips like honey.

"It's no big deal. I'm not much of a cook either, but the grill is the manly man's kitchen," and I wink at her, not wanting her to feel bad.

I see her shoulders relax as she watches me start the grill. While we wait for it to heat up, I feel my warm sensation, and it's not from the wine. She looks cute in her short shorts and tank top. She's not wearing a bra, and I'm tempted to skip dinner and make a meal out of her.

Once the grill is hot enough, I toss the steaks on it and

refill our wine glasses. Rachel tells me about her day and mentions a call from her mother.

"I talked to my dad, too. He's also upset at not being at the wedding and asked if he will be a grandfather."

When Rachel hears this, she falls silent. I'm sure a shotgun wedding never crossed her mind.

Our families are disappointed about not knowing who we married or why it happened so fast. It doesn't help that we cannot erase their doubts or answer their questions.

Rachel mentions hearing from Charlotte, and it sounds as if her sponsors may want her back sooner than expected. My name recognition has something to do with Rachel's profit potential.

I bet as soon as her visa is cleared up, she will fly home and return to her old life in Canada. I don't blame her. It's where her best friend lives and the life she knows, but I don't want any part of that always being on camera 24/7.

This arrangement has an expiration date, so it's only a matter of time before she leaves. Why should she be any different from my mother? I don't want to get hurt again. I need to be prepared for the inevitable.

But, for now, we eat the hot steaks I finished on the grill.

Dinner and dishes done, we retire to the living room. After some TV channel surfing, we find a mafia series we both like, and I slip my hand in hers as we watch the show.

I love the fact she doesn't talk while watching it. Ashley talked non-stop. It's probably a side effect of constantly building her brand and expanding her contacts. Even though we didn't live together, her incessant talking became a deal breaker. I like to hit the off switch when I get home.

Rachel yawns. I mentioned it was time for bed. I have an early morning, but she knows the night is not over. As much as I try to hold back, I'm addicted to everything about her. The way she touches me, the way she makes my heart race and my cock grow stiff. The fact that dinner wasn't cooked like a pro doesn't faze me. She's making an effort. That's all that counts. She must like me because she tries to make our home life comfortable.

Part of me hopes she can't fix her visa and she gets stuck here because I don't want to come home to a house without her in it.

The other part of me wants to bolt before she can leave me.

26

———

RACHEL

I suck at cooking. Blake makes it out to be no big deal. I love that about him. He doesn't sweat the small stuff I obsess over. I constantly beat myself up over my imperfections, and the overachiever in me is hard to control.

As much as I blame my isolated childhood on my parents, I can't blame everything on them. Life is full of setbacks. I'm sure Blake has had a few himself. He avoids talking about his mother, and I catch him dodging her phone calls. Until he resolves those issues, I doubt he can totally commit to any woman. Maybe that's what Ashley knew, and I had to figure it out for myself.

Ashley warned me, and I've been on the lookout for Blake's commitment issues. I love him. His touch sets me on fire like no man before. I worry he'll dump me as soon as he can.

There's no point in sticking around, so I called the Canadian consulate and took the first available appointment over a month away. By then Blake will be on the road, and maybe returning to my old life won't be that difficult.

Charlotte calls. "Have you gotten your sponsors back?"

"Looks like it. But it's Blake's name they want. Not me." Charlotte knows better than anyone my need to be successful on my own merits and not for who I know.

"You're good at promoting their makeup, so of course they want you, and I suppose the new last name doesn't hurt. What are you going to do? Are you coming home anytime soon?"

"I have to meet with Canadian officials in eight weeks to straighten out my visa. What did you think of my novel?"

"I loved it; it's edited; I couldn't stop reading it. The sex scenes were amazing, by the way, you little minx."

"Not because of me, but I'll take it. Do you think the book will get an agent? I'm not looking forward to returning to my old job. Like Blake, I want to do what I love. I want to write books."

"The Blake factor, huh? It sounds like you're attached to him. It comes through in your writing. You're in love with him, Rachel."

Fuck.

"Really?"

"From where I'm sitting, yeah, and you're glowing. I think you're happy there, Rachel. This fake marriage thing might work out. People grow on each other sometimes."

"He dated a model. I met her. She's gorgeous. I've seen some of the teammate's wives. Most of them married their high school sweetheart or are famous in their own right. Very few marry someone ordinary."

"Ordinary meaning not standing there with a bag of millions? Are you feeling sorry for yourself?"

"No. . . oh hell, yeah, I guess I am."

"Look, learn how to cook, clean, pick up his dry cleaning, all those things that make you indispensable. Make sure he notices. Does he come straight home from the arena?"

"Yeah."

"Still fuck you silly?"

"Yeah."

"Then I think you two have a fighting chance. Don't give up before you've given it your best shot."

Pfft. Best shot.

"I'll have to think about that."

"You do that and get your hair done at an expensive salon. Get a massage and get started on your next book."

"Okay." We blow each other a kiss over the video call and hang up.

I'm so screwed. I committed cardinal rule number one and fell in love with my fake husband. Charlotte warned me not to fall in love, but there were sparks from the moment we met. I didn't stand a chance. What woman wouldn't swoon at the site of those sculpted biceps and a cock the size of my forearm?

Enough of this. I have work to do. I go online and make appointments with two different nutritionists; one is Adam, and the other is a bodybuilder named Monique. I meet with Monique first. I find her to be intelligent and well-qualified. But she's also very pretty, and I don't need a temptress meeting with my man every week.

He said to hire who I like, and Adam is just as qualified. He works for other athletes on the team, and he's easy on the eyes. I have to work with him as well. I need to know what foods to buy and what shakes to make. I'm sure I could pay someone to prepare everything, but I want to learn how to do it for him.

I want to help him stay in top form and not get sick this winter. It's the least I can do, given the fact that I have a swanky roof over my head and a hunk in my bed.

Adam is from Texas, born and bred, and has the accent to

prove it. He worked as an occupational therapist and then went into nutrition. He started with wrestlers, then added hockey players before moving to Maine to be closer to his core clients.

"Yes, ma'am," is fun to hear, and I arranged for him to come by and meet with us later in the week.

~

"Pre-season is here at last," Callie squeals with excitement, sitting beside me in the stands. Emily joins us, catching up on the latest gossip while she checks out my huge, sparkling ring.

"Oh, I see it in your face. You're beaming," Emily says, squeezing my hand.

"Am I?" I must be blushing fifty shades of red.

"Oh, yeah, you have it bad. Alexandre was floored you got married without a word," Callie adds.

"We're so sorry about that. Alexandre has been busy, and we haven't had a chance to get caught up," I deflect.

"What about your honeymoon, Callie?" I ask, changing the subject.

Emily is all ears as we listen to Callie and watch the pre-season game. Our guys mostly sit on the bench because pre-season doesn't count in the stats, so they let the rookies and younger guys have a crack at proving themselves.

Still, sitting in the arena knowing my husband is on the ice is incredible. We're in the third period, and Blake goes in. I've never cheered for my man other than my brother. My heart is in my mouth, wanting him to make a goal.

"Look, Rachel, Blake's playing well," Callie points out between sips of her soda. "Alexandre is left-wing, Blake is on the right, so the coach is trying him out for the first line,"

Callie explains as she gives me an excited slap on the back. Callie does the stats for the team, so she knows her stuff.

"I'm sure Blake is happy. He has high hopes for this season."

"Hey, when are the guys drinking beer to toast Paul Newman?" Emily asks.

"I think Alexandre already did that on our honeymoon," Callie jokes, and we all laugh over it.

It's a tradition that started at Longfellow University in Lewiston, Maine, whereby the students drink on campus in September in honor of Paul Newman's line in a 70s movie, "24 hours in a day, 24 beers in a case."

"Yeah, and it caught on at other private universities, and the students go as far as drinking beer in class. Can you imagine?" Emily explains.

"Guess we learn something new every day. I haven't been in Maine long, but it looks pretty."

"Just wait until winter hits. I'll ask you if you still think it's pretty after the white snow turns to dirty slush that sticks around for months."

"I'm from Canada, so that's nothing new. I need to get my winter clothes before it gets cold enough to snow." And then it hits me; I don't know if I'll still live here this winter, and all my cold-weather clothes are in Quebec.

"You must have the best winter outfits," Callie remarks.

"Yeah," I jest, "it's all still in Canada."

"No doubt you'll want to get new stuff anyway. The guys might have a few days off here and there. We need to make the best of it. Maybe we can meet up with them in Colorado for some winter sports," Emily suggests.

"I'll be so big with the baby by then," Callie says, "I'm not going anywhere."

I breathe a sigh of relief when the attention is off me.

How long can I keep this up? I love to hang out with my family and friends, but what if the truth gets out?

I cheer for Blake as he takes a shot on goal and scores. I feel an adrenaline rush almost as exciting as his touch.

We ended up beating the Nashville Legends 3-1. The rookies are proving themselves on the ice. Tonight's winning game is a promising start, but it's only a prequel for the season as the coach tries new line combinations.

We leave the rink, and Callie is too tired to go out. The guys will need time to ride the bike machines to reduce the lactic acid in their legs, plus shower, so there is no reason to wait around.

I head home, and it's with mixed emotions. How can I fix this situation? There is no easy way out of deceiving our friends and family. We're locked in a lie that has gone from a quick fix to my problem.

Not that Blake is innocent. He started this mess by lying to Ashley about us being a couple. From then on, there were rumors about us being together, and it's snowballed ever since.

But how does Blake feel now that we're living a lie daily? Returning to Canada might allow me to process where I am and what I want while searching for answers.

27

BLAKE

Viktor, our captain, tosses me a beer. "Good shot, man, glad you're here. LA wasn't the right system for you to reach your potential. I think you'll do just fine here."

"Thanks, man." That he is watching my plays and commending me goes a long way, as we all thrive on an 'attaboy' attitude. Who doesn't appreciate positive feedback?

"See you soon for that commercial. Bring your pretty boy face. It sells tickets and products," he teases.

"Sure thing." The team captain is the bridge between the players and management when needed and the one who defends us when the refs make bad calls. Most teams have one C for captain, and A, for alternate, but it can be one Captain and four alternates. What the locker room wants is what it gets, as long as we agree.

Like games, we might have all offensive players out there, depending on the team we're playing and their style of setting up plays. Hockey is fun for the fans, but it's pretty fucking complicated living in a system where so many decisions are made for us.

When we're injured, we have to put our faith in the team doctor's treatment plans. How many years we can stay in the game and the quality of life after we retire depends on these doctors' decisions.

The NHL has deemed numerous hits illegal after all the head trauma and spinal injuries over the years. That's why any head injury from an intentional hit, especially a blind-sided hit, will result in a game suspension in addition to the time served in the penalty box. Even if it was an accident, we're punished.

"Hey, wanna grab some brewskis afterward?" Alexandre asks.

"Sure." It would be stupid to say no, although I dread where the conversation will lead. We haven't had a chance to talk about how his sister and I got hitched so quickly, and I have to answer for that eventually.

Fuck. Life didn't seem this difficult when we were on the island. Was it the bewitching waters? Or was it a pocket-size blonde with an independent streak who flashed those cold Nordic eyes at me and softened my heart? I empathize with her situation, especially her need to get out from under her brother's shadow and succeed.

She doesn't have to be famous to be successful. I'm sure she'd be happy with enough money to pay her bills and have a little something left over each month. It's the American dream.

I play with tons of foreign players, and believe me, they love being here, especially the Eastern European guys who had to get approval to leave their home country and pay tons of money to buy their freedom essentially.

I want to help Rachel to succeed. By staying with me, she has a chance to write and see if she can make a go of it. Her book is a secret, and I'll keep it that way. I understand the value of loyalty and know first-hand how difficult it is to come by.

The locker room is clearing out. I follow Alexander to a local watering hole called Sticks and Pucks. It's nowhere near the arena, so we're not likely to bump into any fans, so we'll have some privacy.

The place has Maine written all over it between the dark wood and the requisite moose head hanging above the restroom sign, Bulls for the men and Cows for the ladies. The walls are covered with Maulers autographed memorabilia because the place is owned by Greg, the team's owner, and a few of his cronies. He owned this place before he bought the team.

"How is Greg as an owner?" I ask.

"No complaints—yet." He smiles, and I relax.

My worst nightmare is that he will give that big brother speech and threaten to kick my ass if I don't treat his sister right.

I expected the "you fucked my sister, now I'm going to fuck you" speech, but being married and not just dating her might have saved me. It's hard to tell.

The word is that Alexandre is not only a great player but more of a team player since he met Callie, which helps the team stay cohesive.

To have a championship team, you need a grandstander who puts the team above all else and gives it their all on every play. Is that Alexandre? I don't know yet, but this year has to do much better than last season.

That was a big selling point motivating me to come to this team. The team is solid, but they have some weaknesses that, with their vision and new key players will be fixed. I think our odds are good. I think I'm in a better position than if I was still with the LA Thunder. But then again, one never ever knows. It's not a science. More than a few sportscasters share my view, and I'm expecting a good season with the Maulers.

I text Rachel. *I'm out with your brother, don't stay up for me.*

She's concerned, and I text her. *It's going well.*

Alexandre goes to the bar and returns with two bourbons.

"So, I have a brother-in-law, and, as luck would have it, you play on my team. I can't believe it. I asked Rachel to babysit the house, not fraternize with the new team player."

"We're neighbors. We were bound to run into each other."

"Congrats to you." He raises his glass, and we clink them.

"And to you. I hear Rachel is going to be an aunt."

"Yes, it's fucking amazing. I never dreamed I'd be so excited about having a kid. A little human that will no doubt give me sleepless nights," he grins, "I'm sure I'll love every minute of it."

"You didn't date long either." I try to stave off any further questions about my relationship with Rachel.

"No, we did not. But I'm older than you, and once you're in your thirties and someone turns your head, it makes you see things differently. For me, it was a game-changer. Callie had me from the start. She had backbone and ethics. Much to my amazement, I like a woman who knows her mind." He sips his bourbon and plays with his glass.

Watching him, I'm dying to know what he's thinking. Was it their first date when he felt his heartstrings being pulled? Did his heart race? How did he know it was love? I'd love to ask him, but coming for a newlywed man would sound weird. I should have all that figured out by now.

"So, you two happy? I could run the bullshit, but I want to know my sister is happy and taken care of."

"Oh, hell, man, yeah. I'm not an asshole," I say in my defense.

He's quiet, looks into his glass, picks it up, and finishes the last sip. "Great, because you're going to be an uncle soon, and it's nice to know we have family so close."

"Sure. I'm renting the house until I feel solid with the Maulers. Then I'll buy something."

"Good thinking. I think the team plans on a long-term deal. It's the shit with salary caps and the GM who has to make those decisions every year."

"I understand. It's never easy. Like, we can't just play." I chuckle and toss back the last of my bourbon.

We order appetizers and burgers and watch the hockey games on the big screen TV. I have a nice evening, and he insists on picking up the tab at the end.

I'm relieved he wasn't more inquisitive, but seeing as he rushed into marriage and a baby, he might understand matters of the heart.

My greatest fear is I'll let Rachel down. It's a responsibility to be in a committed relationship; however, that old familiar pull makes me want to run or push her away. I hate how vulnerable I am with her.

I'm uncomfortable, but I can't pull the plug. I have to have her smile and the warmth of her body next to mine at night. The vulnerable part exposes me to the same pain I felt as a teenager. Maybe, it's time to face it, deal with it, and let it go so I can finally be free of the past that grips me from the mysterious beyond called my past.

I don't know how to do that, and there is no way I can share this with anyone other than my dad.

28

RACHEL

Adam, the nutritionist, arrives to finally meet Blake before he hits the road. I've been working with him and learning so much about building muscles that he's motivated me to join a gym.

After sitting on my ass all day plotting my stories and typing away, I need to start exercising before I look like a frumpy wife. I see the competition at the arena and on Blake's social media. At this point, I'm paranoid that if I gain 5 pounds, I might not get invited to events with Blake. It may not be considered politically correct, but the fear is real.

My anxiety about paying my bills has been replaced with concern about fitting in and keeping up with this new crowd. Every day I get phone calls from charities asking for donations and to volunteer my time.

When I married Blake, we never discussed whether I would continue to be his assistant, fielding his calls and making these decisions. His brief take on it was that it would be absorbed by his new wife, agents, and Mauler staff. I stopped answering unknown caller ID numbers after I was told he was not allowed to do any charity work unless it was sanctioned by corporate.

However, in things regarding our life and Blake's health and needs, I'm in it to win it. So, Adam and I are in the kitchen, laughing about the mess I made when I turned on the blender without the lid. He's wiping protein shakes off my face when Blake strolls in.

"Hey there, Blake." They shake hands.

"Adam, nice to meet you. How's the schedule working out for you?"

"Good, I wanted to know if I should up my protein if I'm going to increase my weights, and how much would that be?"

Adam does some calculations and gives him the answer.

"Great, and I like vegan shakes, but it's not the same as real meat. I hate kale too," he adds.

"I'll find alternatives."

I jump in with my questions. "Do you know of a personal trainer for me? I'm new to working out and want to know what I have to do to look like the other WAGS."

"You're perfect, babe. You have nothing to worry about. The world we live in is too obsessed with looks."

Adam gives me a nod; he'll give me a name.

"We're doing pretty well,. I get up early to make Blake his shake, and then I go back to bed. I've never been a morning person," I explain, and Blake clears his throat as if to correct me.

I look at him. "Really?"

Is he implying the morning sex? Is he jealous of Adam?

Adam is great, but he's not Blake. For as long as this lasts, I'm true to my vows and would never cheat or even flirt.

"Never mind," he caves, knowing better than to make problems where there are none.

Why is he cranky? He's not the moody type. He's the shoot-from-the-hip honest type, like his midwestern country roots. He's on the first string like he wanted, so he should be on top of the world.

We wrap it up with Adam, and I confront Blake.

"Are you okay? You're moody, that's not you." I leave out the part about us not exactly tearing up the bedroom every night. Is he distancing himself from me? Is he over being fake married?

"Fine, why?" He's in his cross trainers and workout gear and heading to the gym.

"Things have been off between us. I only have two weeks before I fly to Canada, is that it? Are you nervous about immigration?"

"Yes, no. I gotta go." His car warms up in the garage. He turns to head out and he's gone, the door shutting behind him. Just like he's shutting me out with a big ol' door only it's become a fortress because the walls are so high.

I don't get it. This is why I stayed single for so long. I don't get men. I don't get the games, the mood swings, or the fact that he can't throw his stinky workout shirts in the hamper instead of on the floor. Sometimes, I want to hire a maid instead of being treated like one.

I go to the office I set up in the spare bedroom to work on my next book. I don't know how long I'm in there before I hear the front door open.

"Rachel," Blake hollers.

I come running out, thinking he's hurt and needs me.

"I'm sorry I was an ass in front of Adam," he apologizes, handing me a pumpkin-shaped vase full of mixed daisies, my favorite. He must have gone to a florist to get purple and white flowers added, the team colors.

"I hope you like them." He moves closer, and one whiff of his cologne has my lady parts throbbing; I want him so bad.

"Thanks," I say, rising on my tippy toes to give him a quick kiss, not wanting to force him into more if he's not into it. He places the vase on the nearest flat surface as the kiss deepens and we're peeling the clothes off each other on our way to the bedroom.

Whatever he had going on seems to have slipped back into the shadows. An hour later, he asks me to dress for a nice dinner and evening in town.

"A date night?"

"Sure." He gives me a grin that would melt an iceberg in Alaska.

I run into the other bedroom to pick out a dress to wear later and return to our bedroom.

"You know, I'm a jerk. Hire a closet person to come and build out your side. I never thought about it, but some of my stuff can be moved into another room."

Who is this man? What changed in the last hour? I tell myself not to overthink it. Charlotte will decipher it for me tomorrow.

Blake runs out to finish his training, and I wrap up work myself. When his car returns, my heart has palpitations, and I chalk it up to anxiety over landing an agent for my book.

Blake and I head to our favorite restaurant with its view of the city skyline. From there, we hit club after club. I'm careful to pace my drinking. I want to remember all the details of this perfect night. There may not be many more if immigration dicks me around. One can never be sure of those outcomes.

Could Blake be hiding feelings for me that he hasn't expressed? He keeps his emotions close to his vest, and I can't push him. That never works for anyone. I'm old enough to know that much.

"So, what do you think of Maine?" he asks as we're on our last drink.

"I like it. I have the girls, which is more than I have back home. The days you're on the road are lonely, but I have my writing to work on. Charlotte has my book with an agent, but that could take years."

"That's amazing! You have an agent! Is there any other way to get it out?"

"Self-publishing. I'm not worried. One way or another, it will get out. It's a long way to go for success. It always takes some time unless one is incredibly fortunate, which I am not." I finish my dry red wine and place my empty glass on the bar top.

"Can I help?

"I imagine if I put your last name on it and advertise it that way, it will sell like hotcakes, in theory, but I don't want to do that."

"It's your name, too. I don't mind. It's not like you're using me. . ."

"Look, if we were the real deal, maybe, but I don't feel right about it."

"What if I told you I wanted you to? I want you to be successful. That's all you've ever wanted, and I can give you that."

"You have a point."

"I do," he says, puffing out his chest like he's proud of me and supports my career.

How did I get so lucky?

However, he didn't change my mind one bit. I know it's

okay to ask for help, and Charlotte is doing as much as possible with her contacts. I don't want to look like a desperate homemaker and have the media, and WAGS, say I used my husband to get ahead.

29

BLAKE

Rachel drives my Charger to drop me off at the airport, and she's cracking up listening to the Hillbilly Weatherman on the radio. I crack up because she's just losing it, and when we look at each other, we crack up even more.

"Owe be gosh," she mimics him, trying to sound like a real Mainer. Not a chance with her French, Quebec accent.

"Don't give up your day job."

"I won't. I know I suck at sounding like I'm from Maine. I love the way Callie speaks— less slang and more laid back."

"She's not spewing curse words all the time, either."

"True."

Today hockey season starts and is the first of many long road trips. We'll have four games, and I'll be gone for seven days. Rachel will be in Canada by the time I get home.

I watch her drive, and I want to make love to her again before I go to make sure she remembers me. She's feisty when she needs to be, especially when she calls me on my shit.

I experienced weird pangs in my chest when I walked in on Rachel and Adam having fun in the kitchen. I want to be the only guy who makes her laugh or wipes protein milk off her face. I admit it's selfish and insecure, but that's how I see it. I trust her. I don't know if I trust another man. I'm sure Adam is a great guy, but most men are dogs.

Rachel is perfect. She prepares the meals Adam recommends for me, and she's been working out at the gym with a new trainer. I don't worry about them because she's not the type to compromise our cover by cheating. If I had any doubts, I'd check on them, but she'd see right through me and be insulted.

My hands are all over her when we're together, and I feel the muscle she's gained. She bought some new clothes, not super expensive, but tailored to show off her boobs and full, round ass. I never think about other women when I wrap my arms around her waist. Not that I was thinking of any to begin with, which confuses me even more.

I think of her when I'm supposed to be running a play at practice and get yelled at once for not paying attention. I'm not used to this happening. Rachel is throwing my mind off the world's axis, like a lunar eclipse fucking up high tides, or in my case, missing pucks.

And why would I want to come home to anyone but Rachel? We haven't spoken about her visa because I'm afraid she'll fix it and find a way out of the marriage, which means she'll be leaving me sooner than expected. All I know is that things will go better for her if I were there. But I'm torn.

I thought we'd have a year or two together before we had to make any big decision about our future. But she's young and pretty and probably has other plans. She might have thought this would only be a six-month affair. However, immigration and marriages are a two-year minimum, aren't they?

Rachel parks in front of the terminal, gets out, and walks around my Charger. She loves driving my car and exceeding the speed limit. I smile, knowing it's just a matter of time before she gets a ticket. I tell her they don't mess around in Maine, I tell her, but the girl has a need for speed. Sounds like me.

She leans against the car. "I won't see you until I get back," she says, looking up through her lashes. "I'll miss you, really miss you."

"I'll miss you too, Writer Gal." I bend down to give her a long, deep kiss. This will be the last time I see her for a week. My gut tells me my last name has worked its magic, and that gives way to angst that she might not come back at all. She has meetings with reps in Canada and her social media sponsors who want her back. It's the independence she's been missing since I met her.

"Y'know. . . I never got to see your finished book."

She blushes.

"Is it racy?"

"Oh, yeah." Her smile melts me. I don't want to get on that plane. I'm worried about her traveling alone, and my stomach is in knots, knowing she won't be there when I get home. "Hey, have a safe flight and kick some ass out there. I'll be watching you. Text me. I'm always here."

Does she mean that, or is it another way of softening the blow and saying, 'I'm getting out of this as soon as I cross the border'? Being a jock, normally I wouldn't care, but this is one of the good ones, a keeper. For the second time in my life, she's a woman who has the power to tear my heart out. My mom was first, and Rachel might be the second capable of breaking my heart. Only Rachel doesn't know it.

I give her one more kiss and pick up my bag.

"Be safe, promise me."

"I will. Now get those biscuits in the basket," she hollers as I walk away, and I crack up. She's got the hockey talk down pat.

Looking over my shoulder, I watch her get behind the wheel. She looks good in the Charger. Damn, I should have bought her one of her own. She's been driving my old truck and never complains about the air conditioning not working and the window that's a pain in the ass to roll up and down.

She's not into me for the things I can buy her—clearly.

What took me so long to figure all this out?

But when it comes to our marriage, how do I know when she's acting and when she's not? Hell, my mother didn't want me. Why would Rachel? She's got her shit together. I don't know why men aren't lined up to ask her out. Guys always check her out when we're together, but then they see me and back off.

Rachel has this aura of purity about her that draws people in. She doesn't seek them out. Good people find her and identify with her. With her on my arm, I look and feel better than when I'm alone.

Alone.

That's now a lonely word. Do I want to be alone again and date more Ashleys? Women who want all the benefits and put in none of the work. Women who pick fights and fuel arguments when I'm cranky. Unlike Rachel, who lets me know I can't talk to her that way even if I'm grumpy, and she waits for me to fix my attitude. She's the lovely woman I fell for in St. Bart's when she handled the Make a Kid Smile event with class.

I board the team's plane and sit next to Finn for a front-row seat to Viktor's pep talk. We're heading west to play the

Vegas Bobcats. We'll stop in Colorado to play the Bears. Then we hit Minnesota for the game against the Mayhem and flew out to Vancouver to play the Cougars.

I send Rachel a cute text before we take off.

We check into our hotel in Vegas, and it's time to eat and rest before we play our game at six p.m.

I'm sharing a room with Simon. He became my first friend here as we both came on over the summer. Then, I met Rachel and haven't had much time to catch up with him since. I ask how he and his young daughter are doing.

Thankfully everyone is okay, and we talk some hockey before we catch a nap before the game.

With the game starting at six p.m. it's nine p.m. Rachel's time, and I wonder if she'll be watching. I hate time changes. Our internal clocks are always messed up, so we try to get sleep when we can and always before a game.

I'm stoked Alexandre and I are on the same line. We take to the ice with the deafening roar of the fans in our ears. This is a tough arena, and we won't be able to hear much on the ice.

The first period starts fast, we're competitive, and it's like a tennis match with us bouncing back and forth. We catch some changeovers in the slot, and the Vegas team times it right to pick off a pass and gets a shot on a goal that slides in under Luc's nut sac. Fucking five-hole.

Damn, I hate those, but I'm sure Luc hates them more. My shift is over. The momentum is now with Vegas. The fans are going crazy and shouting, "McDavid, you suck."

Kal, the alternate captain, is the one to give us the pep

talk on the bench. He's trashing the other team, trying to keep us psyched up and putting wind in our sails.

He's great with one-liners, but we're professionals and can't laugh. He manages to make us feel better about going back out there and getting our bodies slammed in what turns out to be a very physical game.

Justin Puljuiar, our toughest and largest player, snorts smelling salts before he heads out. When Kal gets a bad hit, Justin shoves the Vegas player hard, and then, of course, the guy has to retaliate. It's game on, and the first fight of the night ensues. Justin ends up pulling the jersey over the opponent's head, and it's so ugly that both players get five minutes in the sin bin.

But it's got us fired up.

Fuck. But at least it's still 4 on 4 and we don't have to play shorthanded.

The evening wears on, and Finn scores a goal. After a celly on the ice, he swings by the bench for the gloved fist bumps of his teammates.

I'm up and can't think of anything but the game as I give it my all. I get lucky. The puck takes an awkward bounce off the Vegas guy's skate, and I tap it behind the goalie. He had no shot at making the save.

It was a battle we fought well and won 5-4.

With game one on the road behind us, we fly out late and arrive in Colorado at 2 in the morning. I text Rachel that I'm in the hotel but know she's asleep. At least she'll know I was thinking of her.

The problem with playing against the Colorado Bears at their arena is that the elevation is a ball buster. We never have time to acclimate to it, so we will be sucking fumes for the game.

I sleep thinking of Rachel and wonder what's going on

with her. My heart is breaking with the notion she might not return.

In the morning, the team eats breakfast in the hotel conference room so we're not disturbed by fans who may recognize us. My phone vibrates. It's Rachel, and my heart skips a beat, which is insane. Men's hearts don't do that.

I blame it on the altitude and return her text. We go back and forth about the game. She says she was home and watched the entire game. And she jumped and screamed when I scored.

That must mean something.

Maybe she loves hockey?

30

RACHEL

I watched the Colorado game, and the loss did not surprise me. The high altitude makes for a home-team advantage. I've watched enough hockey to know it comes up every year during the playoffs. The Western division teams play very physical hockey, and if Colorado is their final game in the semifinals, the visiting team is a goner before the first period is over.

The loss wasn't an issue. The season doesn't hinge on one game this early in the season. However, by the three quarters mark, every game is vital for ranking as it sucks to be a wild card going into the semifinals. That's when shit gets very real. Teams can be swept out of contention in the first round, and no one knows which wild card will unseat a top-tier team.

I love the excitement of the final leg of the run for the Cup, and I get frustrated that I can never pick the Stanley Cup winner. There is no way to predict when wild shit happens. Players get injured, sometimes intentionally, as they get hurt trying to eliminate a good player and increase their chances of winning.

I hate that part. It's not fair. It's downright dirty. I love hockey, but not the career-ending nasty hits that come with it. I worry Blake will be receiving one of those, so I was on pins and needles when the game got rough tonight. After Blake was shellacked into the boards, and it wasn't called, I texted him to see if he was okay.

It took him a while to get out of the arena, but he finally texted and said he was bruised but he'll be fine.

The player that hit you better be happy I wasn't there, I reply.

I remember, as a kid, being scared for my brother when he took hits, but we both got used to it. It's the price he pays to do what he loves. It looks pretty freakin' painful if you ask me.

We exchange a few texts, and he says he has to eat and get some sleep.

After we say goodnight, I begin packing for my trip home tomorrow. Seeing Charlotte and my parents are the highlights compared to my immigration interview. I'm not looking forward to answering 5,000 questions from the parents, but I owe them a visit. I only have a few pictures of the wedding to show them. The Maulers wanted engagement pictures for their website, but we got busy with preseason and never had a chance to arrange a photoshoot.

Knowing Charlotte is always up late, I call her on my way to the kitchen for a bowl of ice cream.

"What's up? I'm picking you up tomorrow, right?"

"Yes, you are, and you know it. Don't play that 'I forgot about you' game, missy," I tease. She might be older than me, but I can still give her shit.

"Any word on the book?"

"Not yet, but bad news comes fast. Don't worry, you may get picked up. You've worked for a newspaper, and since you're so good with social media, you're like a racehorse in the Breeders Cup."

"I'm not."

"You better think you are. It's called the power of positive thinking."

"Great. Anything new with you?"

"Your room is a bit of a mess. I have too much clutter, so I'm trying to get rid of stuff."

I choke on my spoonful of rocky road.

"What? You? You've never been able to get rid of anything with a designer label on it."

"I know, but I'm trying. Plus, I put on a few pounds dating lover boy. That man is as good in the kitchen as he is in bed."

"Wow, things do change," I marvel. She usually lives on a starvation diet, so this new guy sounds like a healthy influence.

"Okay, I better go. We can talk more tomorrow."

"Right, love ya."

"Love ya back."

~

The team left Colorado. Blake is in Minnesota for the game today. Callie is driving me to the airport. It's expanding into one with international flights as Camden is in the running for a football expansion team.

She says, "We should have watched the game together last night. It's so cool seeing our husbands on the same line."

"Sounds like fun. We'll have to get Emily involved and rotate houses for the games that aren't televised too late."

It's starting to feel like I have a new family with the team.

While the guys are on the road, the women must get lonely, and we should stick together.

We make it to the airport, and Callie hugs me before she drives away. With only a carry-on, I head straight to security. Fingers crossed, I don't get stuck in Canada. That would really suck. My attorney said not to worry, but I'm still nervous. Everything would be better if Blake were here, but I don't want to bother him during his season.

The flight is short, and as soon as I exit the airport, I see Charlotte pull up. She jumps out of her car and hugs me like it's been years instead of months. She chats away as we listen to a Quebec radio station featuring local bands.

It's good to be home but weird at the same time. I have a better understanding of what the players must go through between games, traveling, and the emotions that come with trying to juggle home life and families.

"Blake will be in Vancouver tomorrow. They have a day off after they play the Nashville Legends. That puts him home before me."

"So, how is Blake? You lucky girl."

"Yeah."

"Oh, my god, I forgot to look at your ring." She grabs my hand with the sparkling platinum setting filled with brilliant diamonds. "It's stunning. That boy loves you."

"Then why won't he say it? I'm not going first. You know the code." I sound angry, and it's misdirected. "Sorry," I mumble.

"It's fine. You're frustrated. From what you've told me, he had a fucked-up childhood. Since then, he has dodged commitment like the plague and may never tell a woman he loves her. Divorce does that to kids."

"I'm beginning to think every kid has a fucked-up childhood. I'm still mad at Alexandre for scaring off the boys throughout high school. Good intentions, my ass."

"He didn't do it with malice. He thought he was protecting you. It's what brothers do, and it's in the past."

"Yeah." I perk up as she parks in front of our apartment. "It's over, and nothing compared to the adult things I have to worry about."

"That's the spirit," she chirps, unlocking the door to our apartment.

It's surreal returning to the home I left a few months ago. It feels more like a lifetime.

"What's up with the sponsors?" Charlotte asks.

"I put a pin in that for now, but I have to give them an answer soon."

"Cup of tea?" she offers.

"Sure." The temperature outside is in the sixties, but tea is our thing.

She boils the water and makes us black tea as I wheel my carry-on to my bedroom. So much has happened since I was in this room last. I look around and take a few minutes to stuff items that no longer fit into my new life in the bags Charlotte left on my old bed.

"What's up with your visa?"

"I have a meeting with them tomorrow afternoon while Blake is flying to Vancouver for his last game on this long road trip."

"Both on opposite sides of the country, eh?"

We sit on the sofa, and I hold my teacup between my palms as if to warm them. I'm not cold, but I do find it relaxes me.

"I don't know what to do, Charlotte. I love my life. I'm happy."

"You're in shape, that's for sure," she says, eyeing my arms and trim waist.

"I've been going to the gym and eating healthy, like Blake. His meals are specifically designed for him, so I benefit too. I hired a cute guy as his nutritionist, and I think Blake got pissed." I snicker.

"Really? Why?"

"There's no way I'm going to dangle some smoking hot chick under my husband's nose. I trust Blake, but a man is just as qualified."

"You made Blake jealous."

"Not intentionally. Blake told me to hire someone I could work with, and I did. Trust me, if Adam weren't good, he'd be fired, but Blake actually likes him now that he's used to him. Plus, Adam gave me the name of an excellent trainer at the gym who kicks my ass."

"You've been busy. No wonder I don't hear from you."

"Text me any time." I lean forward and hug her. "I've missed you."

"Same here. It's too quiet without you. So, what are you going to do? The marriage, the visa, the job?"

"Hm, well, Blake told me to use my married name for the book if it helps to sell and promote it. But I don't want to depend on him for my success."

"I get it. I'm sure celebrities always meet people who want to take advantage of them. It must be difficult to know who to trust."

"Absolutely. You should have seen St. Bart's. Women outnumbered the men. It should have been a charity auction for women to get dates, but they did pretty good circling the bars and especially the pool. I never saw so many lips with filler and foreheads with Botox in my life."

"How was it? The pictures of the beach and water you sent were incredible. Is the sand that white?"

"Yes, it was amazing. I have no idea how much the trip cost him. The sweetest part was when he signed one of his hockey sticks and gave it to a little girl battling cancer as part of the Make a Kid Smile program."

"I'm impressed." Charlotte sits quietly, listening to me talk.

Funny, I used to be the one waiting to hear of her exploits.

We finish catching up just as my voice gives out from talking so much.

"Let's just chill and watch a rom-com so your voice can recover. I'll make more tea and order some lo mein and crab rangoon."

She knows I love Chinese food.

"Great," I croak out and hope my voice recovers before I talk to Blake as I'm stressed out and my voice is not normal.

"Look, why don't you use Blake's name to see if we can sell your book? That way, you don't have to go back to the traitorous sponsors and cutthroat world of social media. Live with Blake and write the next book in the series. I mean, you're having fun, you look great. You're in love."

"Me?"

I think about the time on the island, the adventurous sex, the rescue on horseback, the problem-solving at immigration, the wedding dress, and the ring....

I loved it. I loved it all. I'm in love with my husband.

"But he doesn't love me."

"That rock you're wearing says otherwise. I mean, he didn't have to do that. And on one of the most expensive islands on the planet. He could have waited until you got back to Maine."

"He wanted the day to be special."

"Yeah, I'm sure did. He didn't want to say anything. It was an awkward situation."

"Yeah, like the nip slip the first night we met."

Charlotte laughs and flips her straight black hair over her shoulder. "For sure, but I think you guys complement each other."

"We're both terrible at remembering hotel room numbers," I snicker, "and I hate stupid paperwork like visas. I had no idea I needed it."

"Mm. Visas are tricky, and Canada runs circles around the U.S."

"You're scaring me now. I have an attorney."

"That will help."

"I think I'll clean up my room a bit and see what I might need to have shipped to Maine."

"So, you're going to stay there?"

"I think I'll take my chances and see where it goes. I love him."

"Fair enough, sometimes you have to fight for what you want. I'll order dinner."

I organize my clothes, making a pile to ship and a pile to toss. I'm torn on the name thing. Legally, it's mine to use. I'll talk to Blake about it again.

Dinner arrives, and we eat while watching our favorite romance movies. I love the American ones better than the British ones.

When Blake's game is on, we watch it together. Hockey has given Charlotte more meaning now that she knows more about our team. Plus, she loves the color purple.

～

My phone dings.

Crap, it's morning already. I lift my phone.

Blake.

Are you still with Charlotte?

Yes, I type.

When is the meeting with immigration tomorrow?

Three in the afternoon. Why?

What's the address?

I type it to him.

Great. Don't talk to anyone until you hear from me.

Okay.

I yell for Charlotte and fill her in on the latest.

"That sounds a bit cryptic."

"He's up to something." For one second, it crossed my mind Charlotte has been very quiet today.

31

BLAKE

After the game in Vancouver, I call my dad as I wait for the rest of the team to show up so we can fly out. My call wakes him up in the wee hours of the morning. He sounds worried when he answers the phone.

I don't blame him. I'm worried about myself. I wonder why I haven't found the right one after all these years and all the women I've been with. I'm beginning to think it's me.

What was it Ashley said I don't communicate? I have commitment issues? Was that it? Hell, I can't remember. I wouldn't be surprised to learn that a part of my brain has checked out after a lifetime of coaches barking orders at me. Call it self-preservation.

"Hey, Dad. How are you?"

"Are you okay? It's dark out." Some dads would be annoyed, but not mine. He'd do anything for his sons. He was a great dad, working long hours at his job selling farm equipment and raising us boys.

"Yeah, yeah. Sorry, don't worry. I just need answers, Dad. I'm just wondering, why did Mom leave? I was a teenager, and I had been so angry with her. Back then, I could only interpret it through the eyes of a teenager. Now I want to see it as an adult."

"Mm. Well, maybe it will help you to know she didn't leave you because she didn't love you. That was never the case, Blake. She had lots of problems, son. She hated living in the country and wanted to move to a big city. She had mood swings that were taking a toll on you kids, so she left to spare you and your brother. She thought a life without drama would give you both a stable environment. I agreed because it was too much work taking care of her issues, two boys who excelled at sports, plus working my job."

"She didn't leave because she didn't love us?" My voice begins to crack, remembering her driving away and running after her, crying for her to stay.

"She loves you boys; it was the hardest decision of her life. She did fly in from time to time to watch you play hockey. She kept her distance to avoid giving you false hopes that she would stay. She always hoped you and your brother would come around when you grew up. I can't make you call her or love her. It's up to you to process it and figure it out."

My heart is broken knowing my mother's sacrifice and the guilt I have for shutting her out all these years. My anger and resentment fade into the backdrop of happier times in my childhood, like her seeing my first goal when I was four and her throwing great birthday parties at the rink. I have all the photos to prove it.

Then the flashbacks kick in of her crying at the kitchen table and me trying to make her feel better with a hug; I must have been seven. There were days she didn't even get out of bed, and I'd slip get-well cards under her door.

Now, it's all coming together like a child's twelve-piece puzzle. How could I have forgotten?

"Thanks, Dad. I love you. I can't tell you how much you

mean to me and how much I love you. I wouldn't be where I am without you."

"It's okay, son. We're good?"

"Yeah, we're great. Get some sleep. I'll see you soon."

"Bring that wife of yours; she looks like a sweet gal, I'd love to meet her."

"Sure thing."

My teammates file out of the locker room and pile into a van to the airport.

I leave a message on my mother's answering machine.

"Mom, if you get this, I love you. I married a great gal, and I'd like you to meet her one day."

I texted Rachel, asking for the immigration information. Then I call her attorney and find out it's an interview and I need to be there. Damnit, Rachel never told me how serious this is. She's stubborn and wants to do everything on her own. I planned on being there but didn't know how much she meant to me until she left.

By no means was it easy flying across the country to arrive in Montreal to hop on another plane to Quebec. I only have two days off, so to recoup, I need to sleep on the plane, but it's hard to do when all I can think about is Rachel and how she's the one who takes care of me and never yells when I leave my dirty clothes on the floor. She takes care of herself and has an independent streak that rivals a homeless child.

I take public transportation to downtown Quebec, asking for directions along the way, which is useless as I don't speak their French, or much French at all, except for a few words Rachel taught me. My GPS is confusing the hell out of me. The red GPS dot would be more efficient as a beacon for ships that need to find the coastline in dense fog. Because for the life of me, I can't seem to find the appropriate building with it.

Turning the corner, I see Rachel, dressed in a suit and heels, standing by a fountain in front of an office building. There's a tall woman beside her, older, with dark hair and dark eyes. That must be Charlotte.

I jog until I reach Rachel and lift her in the air. I'm so happy to see her.

"You're a sight for sore eyes," she teases.

I'm sure I am with a tired face. I run my fingers through my hair as if it replaces the shower I should have taken before showing up.

"Yes, I am. It was a hell of a long flight, I mean flights," but I smile and kiss her long enough to make Charlotte blush and turn away.

I set her down and walked her closer to the fountain.

"Charlotte, join us." I wave for her to follow.

"You know, Rachel wanted you at her wedding. You're the only one who knew our secret."

"I know." She smiles. "I kept it."

"Yes, you did," I nod in appreciation.

Kneeling, I take Rachel's hand in mine.

"Rachel Holloway, I love you. I'm so in love with you. I can't stop thinking about you. Will you marry me? For real, marry me?"

Her eyes tear, and her mascara runs as she can no longer hold back the waterworks.

"I love you, too. I miss you so much when you're gone."

I stand and kiss again as Charlotte applauds and takes pictures with her cell phone.

"Okay, you two love birds, you're making me cry." Charlotte wipes her eyes. "But you're going to be late. Go in there and pass that interview because I can't stand the thought of you guys not being together."

"Good point," I reply as I take Rachel's hand, and Charlotte follows to wait for us in the lobby.

The interview took two hours and consisted of endless personal questions. Thank God we lived together and knew all the answers. We pass the tests, and Charlotte gets a spousal visa with her new married name.

We're leaving the building together when someone recognizes me and takes pictures. I pull Rachel to me, and we pose, smiling. One person leads to more; before you know it, the crowd is overwhelming.

Charlotte is speechless, watching my fans go nuts.

"Wow, that's intense. Do you get that everywhere?"

"If they notice me. I didn't expect to have it happen here." I grin sheepishly. "Charlotte, I want you to put the name Rachel Gibson on her book."

Rachel makes as if she's going to protest, but the words freeze on her lips.

"She's my wife, we're in this together, and I want her to have a bestseller."

"Yes, sir," Charlotte replies with a lighthearted and nervous giggle.

RACHEL'S SUMMATION

Rachel

How the hell can a girl refuse a real proposal after a fake one? To say I wasn't smitten with Blake from the first hookup would be a lie. And we've had enough of those the past few months to last a lifetime.

Blake made peace with his mother and is helping his brother, Sam, do the same. He's in college and old enough to begin processing the facts. Maybe this way he can avoid picking women like Ashley. Fortunately, Blake was able to figure it out in time to salvage our marriage and he dodged all the women who weren't right for him.

Hockey season is in full swing. Tonight is a home game and Emily, Callie, and her BFF, Sarah, are here tonight. Man, is Callie blossoming with her baby belly. It won't be long now.

I am enjoying the box we got at the arena with some of the other WAGS when a woman approaches me. I don't recognize her, but her voice is familiar.

"You must be Rachel," she extends her hand, "I'm Leah, Blake's mom."

She has his hair and skin coloring, and the instant connection sinks in. I didn't tell Blake I invited her in case she didn't show up, but I sent her a plane ticket to come and watch Blake play in his home stadium.

I hug her. "Thanks for coming," I say as I take her by the hand to meet my friends before I lose it and start crying. After hearing her story, I'd fill up Camden Bay with my tears, so I stifle the waterworks and pray to God she stays to see Blake after the game.

Introductions are made, and we all bond over warm pretzels, mustard, burgers, and beers. I hope Blake is okay with finally seeing her after many years.

His game starts slow, and the guys skate like they're wearing cement blocks, but after another grueling road trip out west, I can't blame them. I can, however, blame them for partying too much at our house during an unofficial, late-night wedding reception in which Blake will see his mom when he gets home. They both teared up, but I know my husband finally has closure and so does his mother.

I put her in the guest room and made her comfortable for the night as tomorrow is a big day.

It's noon as friends arrive for the 'real wedding' party. I have to slip out and pick up buns and condiments, and when I open the door to the garage, I see a shiny blue car parked in the garage I glance at the long driveway to see the truck parked at the end of it so we can maneuver cars.

Now I know why he sent me to the mall with Callie the day before.

I'm not a car person, but the emblem on the hood looks familiar.

"It's a Mercedes, I hope you like it," he says, and he slips the key fob into my hand.

"For me?"

"Yeah, that starts the car," he teases. "It's just like Callies to start. But it should be a hell of a nicer ride." He grins, and I throw my arms around him and kiss him profusely.

He's like a kid unwrapping the newest hockey video game. I know because he still loves playing it with his headset on. When I hear his excited voice, I smile because he's enjoying his best life and it's complete now that he's filled in all the pieces of his youth.

"Thank you, my love." I slide my hands further up around his neck and kiss him longer the second time. "It's gorgeous who would have imagined you're such a romantic?"

"Right? I hope we get to stay here a long time because this place is growing on me."

Continue reading with Benched by the Nanny. When the cute bartender needs a ride home and the irresistible hockey player gives her a ride, and it changes her life forever,

LOBSTERFEST BONUS SCENE

We drive up the coast for the anticipated Lobster Fest on Sunday before season starts. There is a group of us who rented a limo to make the two-hour journey up the Maine coast to a fishing community called Holden.

There is plenty of alcohol in the limo, and I opt for champagne. It's nice to be surrounded by couples, Emily and Wyatt, and my brother with Callie. Plus, we have the older veteran, Viktor, with us, along with Colton and Simon. Simon and Viktor are still single, and they give us some flak about being married, but overall, it's been a good ride. The guys talk, and the girls share stories as I take in the beautiful fall day, knowing that the tough part is going to be Blake being on the road.

I'll be alone in our huge house, and I'll plot out a book series, eat too much pizza and potato chips, and binge-watch the *girlie* shows on the main streaming services -no self-respecting jock is going to watch a love story unless it involves fighters, spaceships, or zombie.

The town is tiny, and yet, thousands of people flock here

annually from around the world just to eat fresh lobster from this seafaring town. I hear music; it's vaguely familiar, an old group called *Sister Hazel* is playing familiar tunes.

We take to the streets that are blocked off and join in with strangers who have no clue they walk next to a few Maine's only pro hockey players. It makes me smile that we're getting away without being discovered or stalked by the press as we practically waltz by them and the vats of lobsters boiling. When the lobsters come out, they are placed in netting with boiled potatoes, an ear of corn, a tiny fork, and wet naps.

The price might give sticker shock to some, but it's fresh and we're enjoying the ambiance as the guys split up: those getting beers and those getting our lobsters. We girls grab a table.

"Callie, you're looking great." I observe her glowing face, and I've never seen my brother happier.

"Thanks, sis! So, what do you think of Colton, is there a girl we can set him up with?"

"I don't know anyone."

"One thing is for sure, there's always a new face popping up since Camden Hills has grown so much over the past five. I mean, just north of us is that gorgeous mall."

"Oh, yeah, it's amazing," I add. That's where Alexandre took me shopping for the trip to St. Barts and the fancy lunch on the water.

"How was your trip to St. Barts?" Emily asks. "We never really saw wedding pictures."

"I have only a few. I need to have some professional ones done one of these days. I don't know when we'll have time. Everything was so rushed as it was."

"So, how is married life?" she prods.

"Good, I mean, different. But it's nice to know what

to expect, and I'm taking full advantage of the personal trainer and the nutritionist."

"You look amazing." Callie nods to the guys heading our way.

"Thanks, I have to say this is the best shape I've ever been in." I grin sheepishly. I keep the hot sex comments to myself, and I'm relieved I can share them with Charlotte and not worry about them getting around the team.

Blake told me that some of the women can get a bit chippy, so until I know who my real friends are, I'm keeping details to myself, except for Callie because she's family. *If she's not safe to share my life with— I have bigger issues.*

I find Emily to be sweet. She's from Miami and is an attorney, and her office isn't far from the arena. She works with her old boss, who happens to be Blake and Alexandre's agent, Dan. She's older than Wyatt, but it's not evident as she's pretty, mature, and has a nice personality.

"So, how is your puppy doing?" Callie asks her.

"Mika is great, getting big, y'know? She doesn't understand that her body is huge and knocks over some things, especially her tail."

"Yeah, and the hair, my God," Wyatt exclaims plopping down as many plastic cups of beer that he can carry on the table. They are nicknamed "German Shedders" for a reason. We have to vacuum the walls; the hair is insane."

"Yes, but you love her," Emily teases.

"Of course, I do, she was the glue that kept you here long enough for us to make it official," he says beaming.

Blake and Viktor show up with lobster, and the talk turns to food. I'm at a loss for how to dig into this feast wrapped in a net. Blake takes the lobster and using his hands, cracks open the claws and opens the cups of butter.

"Like this," he says, using the tiny fork to get the meat

out. He pulls a huge lump of meat out of the claw, dips it in the melted butter, and feeds it to me.

"Awe, newlyweds," Viktor coos like a jerk.

I want to say fuck off, but Blake does it for me.

When we've had our fill, we toss our garbage and walk along the road, taking in the independent booths with jams, and something called Maple Butter that all the non-locals are scooping up.

Callie tells me it's great on turkeys and just about anything, but we can get it locally. There is no need to pay inflated prices.

Strolling along, we pass by a person in a huge lobster outfit, one that would be deemed worthy of Halloween, it's so large it has a fan in it to keep the human inside alive.

"How cute," I say.

"I'd love to dip you in butter," Viktor says, just being funny as we pass the lobster. As a response, the lobster moves, shoving a pamphlet stamped with PETA, into his hand.

No fucking way.

I look to Blake. I'm horrified PETA is here. He looks at me, and I roll my eyes as we lock arms and have a private laugh over the fact I lost my influencer accounts over eating beef in public. The irony of them being at this event isn't lost on us.

It seems PETA is protesting the harvesting of Lobsters. It's not that I realize I've been out of the social media scene longer than ever. My days as an influencer are in my rearview mirror.

Funny, I haven't given my old career much thought as I've been busy starting my new life. I love writing all day and have created a routine for when Blake is around. That way, I have time for him and make up my missed writing days when he's on the road. Working keeps me from being depressed that he's not home to snuggle with at night. We found video calls are great and faster than texting. The bottom line is he communicates with me, and I know he's always thinking about me. All in all, I'd say life is pretty good right now.

DEDICATION

Dedicated to the Make a Wish Foundation.
Thank you to all the players who grant kids wishes.

TEAM ROSTER

TEAM ROSTER 2021-22 (subject to change)

C-Kal Kohlman #5, "A" Alternate captain as per Jagged Ice.

C- Jacques Bellare #65

C-Austin Martin, pronounces Maratn #38 is his lucky number

C-Eric Thomas #96

C- Finn Callahan #71

RW-Sean Ian #57

RW-Victor Karlsson "C" for Captain #90,

RW-Alexander Holloway #23

RW-Raymond Frick #73

LW- Wyatt Hildebrand #19 nicknames Hildy, Broomhilda

LW- Albert Bennett #86

LW-Sidney Roy #98

LW-Chandler Ross #49

D-Justin Puljujar #55

D-Colton Cermak #62

D- Simone Korhomen #77

D- Blake Gibson #45

D-Trevor Espisito #41 born April 1

D-Devin Coyle #68

G-Luc McDavid #23 f (or Patrick Roy)

G-Jason McKinney, backup #30 which is Martin Brodeur's number.

RESERVES

F-Greg Coture. #87 for Crosby, his idol as a kid

F-Douglas Wright #8 for Ovchekin

F-Michal Mitchell "#94 M&M" "Candy"

D- Georgiev Laurent #82 "Laundry" and at night "Dirty Laundry"

D-Roy Crug # 71 "Croog" is how it's pronounced

NHL TEAMS FOR THE SERIES

The NHL Team list for the Maine Maulers Series *subject to changes

Atlantic Division

Fort Myers Gators (Jackson: Against the Boards is on this team)

Buffalo Blazers

Boston Sharks

Detroit Brawlers

Jacksonville Titans

Ottawa Kings

Toronto Twisters

Wyoming Wolfs

Metropolitan Division

Washington Devils

NJ Bandits

Philly Flames

Carolina Cobras

Montreal Mounties

Nashville Legends

NY Renegades

Central Division

Calgary Oilers

Chicago Blizzards

Colorado Bears (Jackson: Against the Boards)

Dallas Bucks

Pittsburg Rockets

Quebec Pioneers

St. Louis Archers

Vegas Bobcats

Pacific

LA Thunder (Coach: Isak Sin Bin Series)

Edmonton Enforcers

Minnesota Mayhem

Phoenix Diamondbacks (Liam: The Enforcer)

San Diego Defenders

Seattle Whalers

Vancouver Cougars

ALSO BY ZOE BETH GELLER

Buy bundle deals at shopzoebethgeller.com

Tyler: Hooked (Free prequel to the series)

Sin Bin Hockey Series (10)

The Sin Bin Hockey Series

Jackson: Against the Boards

Alan: Between the Pipes

Erik: Fire and Ice

Blayze: Slap Shot

Pavvo: The Defender

Spencer: Penalty Box

Isak: Coach

Kaden: Game Time

Liam: The Enforcer

Jake: Roughing

Sin Bin Series Box Sets (3)

The Sin Bin Hockey Series Box Set Books 1-4

The Sin Bin Hockey Series Box Set Books 5-7

The Sin Bin Hockey Series Box Set Books 8-10

Zoe Beth Geller's Hockey Pond Facebook Fan Group

Maine Maulers Hockey Series

Rookie in Love

Jagged Ice

Hotter than Puck

Benched by the Nanny

Puck in the Oven

Pucking the Team Captain

Pucking with the Goalie

Maine Megaladons Football Series

Faking it with the Football Star

The Player's Obsession

The Dirty Series-Micheli Mafia (5)

Italian King A Dark Mafia Romance Book 1

Dirty Vengeance: A Dark Mafia Romance Book 2

Dirty Bargain: A Dark Mafia Romance Book 3

Dirty Born: A Dark Mafia Romance Book 4

Dirty Deals: A Dark Mafia Romance Book 5

Dirty Series Dark Mafia Facebook Fan Group

Volkov Brava Series

King's Promise

Brutal Promise

Sinful Promise

Borrelli Mafia

Free Prequel: Nanny for the Bodyguard in my store

Mafia King: Matteo

ACKNOWLEDGMENTS

Thank you to everyone who is following me on this journey. I hope you are enjoying this series. Special thanks to my hubby for his support. And as always my besties Mo, Aidy. You all help me so much as you know the author life and how wild it is! Special thanks to Barb for proofreading!

ABOUT THE AUTHOR

Zoe Beth Geller, a captivator of hearts and a master of suspense, crafting mafia romances filled with unexpected plot twists and thrilling surprises. Her literary journey doesn't stop there; she also delves into the vibrant world of sports, creating enthralling hockey and football romances that never fail to score a touchdown or shoot a hat trick with her readers. A proud resident of Southwest Florida, Zoe cherishes the sun-kissed life alongside her loving family. When she isn't weaving romantic tales, Zoe revels in family get-togethers, enjoying the playful company of her two cherished labs, and indulging in a well-brewed espresso. Each story she writes is a passport to adventure.

Stay connected with Zoe through her fan groups and her newsletter with updates on evolving news, teasers, cover reveals, sample chapters, and new releases. If mafia is your jam, you can find her fan groups on Facebook.

Facebook Fan Groups
Zoe Beth Geller's Hockey Pond
ZBG Dark Mafia Romances

Follow me on TT at zoebethgellerauthor

facebook.com/zoebeth.geller.96

instagram.com/zoegellerauthor

bookbub.com/authors/zoe-beth-geller